Say You'll Love Me
And Other One Acts

By Sarah Wolf

*There's a darkness upon you that's flooded in light
And I'm frightened by those who don't see it.*

The Avett Brothers

wolfstarpress.com || copyright 2020

Dead in an Hour

She would be dead within the hour, but Maude O'Connor had no idea. She was settling down to watch *Days of our Lives* as she did every weekday afternoon at one o'clock sharp. Plunging her large, flowing frame into the deep cushions of her white leather couch, Maude propped her fat ankles on her glass coffee table and clicked the television on. Another day, another hour lost in the weird spheres of soap opera lives, unreal, unbearable, unlivable. Maude could feel her eyes grow heavy at the first appearance of John Black's twitchy, but shapely, eyebrows on the screen.

She hated John Black.

Which was odd because he was the hero of the show, had been for years. But she'd hated him for years, his spasmodic face, his cocky attitude, his woolly chest, his famous *That's a fact!* tag line. She cheered for the DiMeras, the evil but lovable villains, to take *That'safact* Black out. "But the fans would hate that, Aunt Maude," her thirteen-year-old niece Betsy whined whenever Maude mentioned offing the ogrish hero. *What fans*, she wondered. She was the only fan she knew.

She wasn't really a fan, though. Actually, she hated *Days of our Lives*. She watched it out of respect for Derby, her late husband.

Even that wasn't true, though. Derby hated *Days of our Lives*, abhorred anything remotely literary, like a soap opera. "Too many confangled words," he'd mutter through a cloud of cigar smoke. "Too many people who don't know who they're related to or who they're in love with. It's par-thetic, Maude." He said *par-thetic* often, as if it were a real word. She hated that about him, almost as much as she hated his cigar smoke, the patch he wore over his left eye, and the day he died, leaving her alone in her unattainable misery. She hated him because she couldn't blame him any more. Every day she watched *Days of our Lives* out of respect for the fact that he hated that she watched it every day.

She could blame her grandmother Lorraine for that. She was the one who first introduced Maude to Salem and its intricate web of idiotic love quadrangles, habit of raising inane characters from the dead to read tacky dialogue off a cue card for a few more years until they were killed off again, and other rabid pricks of fun and excitement. Lorraine raised Maude and her brother Pete from the time they were twelve and four, respectively, ever since their father Rutherford left Sutherfield Village to panhandle in Harvard Square and their mother Ruth dyed her blonde hair red and went out West to become a Hollywood actress. On the day her son left her grandchildren on her front porch, Lorraine had stubbed out her cigarette on the door frame and muttered, "Ah, shit." But Lorraine swept Maude and Pete into the house and there they stayed until their eighteenth birthdays, respectively, at which time their grandmother pushed them back out onto the porch and offered this advice: "Shack up with someone who's got money."

Of course, her childhood hadn't been all bad. Outside of the daily grind of *Days of our Lives* and the incessant chattering of Lorraine's African Gray Parrot Luigi, Maude and Pete had many half-seconds of pure adolescent bliss. Every third Wednesday of the month, Rutherford would call his children from a pay phone outside the Harvard Yard. "Dad's gotten some good dough this week," he'd say, his voice tipsy with brown paper bag delight. "Dad made an instrument out of an empty shoe box and a rubber band. Be good for Lorraine," he'd say, and his children, gathered eagerly around the phone clenched in their grandmother's hands, would nod and Pete would drool, as was his custom when he was particularly happy.

Lorraine would hang up the phone, mutter, "Deadbeat," and sit down to watch *Days of our Lives*.

Maude started watching the show as a way to spend time with her grandmother without having to try to find things to say. When she was young, Maude wanted to be nothing like anyone in her family, but she still wanted to make the effort to get along with at least one member. Later, much later, long after Lorraine died from a burst appendix, Maude realized Pete was the one she should have paid the most attention, but by then he was shacked up with Mrs. Lindsay, the richest matron in town, breeding contemptuous offspring such as whining Betsy and the laughably meager twins Kelvin and Kevin, and still a frequent drooler. "That brother of yours should be committed," Derby used to say through hacking coughing fits. "He slobbers worse than Mud," he'd add, pointing an accusatory finger at Maude's mastiff, lazy and drooping in the corner.

Maude never said she agreed with Derby, but she often thought she might. He was, after all, the most consistently negative person in her life, which made him the most reliable person she knew. Nothing ever made him happy, but that only made Maude's duties as his wife that much simpler. And he never lied because he never had a reason to, which made him the one person she could depend on. He was eight years her senior and picked her up off her grandmother's porch two days after she turned eighteen, told her he wore the patch because he'd lost an eye in the war, and took her to a dance at the Y. He was the worst dancer she'd ever seen, except for maybe herself, but he gave her a place to stay besides Lorraine's porch, so she never begrudged his sour attitude. Maybe he'd saved her.

Or maybe he'd ruined her -- if there was anything left to ruin, that is. Maude didn't know and didn't care. When he'd died a year and a half ago, she hadn't cried until she realized that, for the first time in her life, she was alone.

That is, except for her mastiff Cork. Mud had died effortlessly in the heat of July and been replaced by the insolent, disobedient Cork, unruly and only slightly charismatic. By the time Derby finally died, it was March and Maude was tired of wishing Cork was more like Mud and even more tired of *Days of our Lives*. "I swear, Aunt Maude, this dog is dumber then Dumbo Austin," Betsy would whine, writhing and grimacing on the opposite end of the white leather couch. Maude didn't like the comparison of her dog to Austin Reed, once a gloriously handsome boxer/musician who was recast and reduced to bumbling, inarticulate pseudo-executive, but she couldn't refute her niece's charge. Cork was like Austin. Pet rocks had more personality.

Of course, Cork still outwitted Betsy and the Special K twins. Even Betsy admitted that. Pete would bow his head sheepishly, forget to wipe the drool from his chin, and explain that he and Mrs. Lindsay were too busy being shacked up to spend much time with the zygotes they spawned. *Spawned* was Derby's word for it, though, not Pete's. Pete told Maude, "They's my penny pushers," and Maude would frown, blink away her revulsion, and say nothing. Derby always stepped in between them, anyway, and waved a fat finger in Pete's saliva-covered face. "You should be institutionalized," he'd say. Pete would grin, pull Betsy off the leather couch, and head back to Mrs. Lindsay's house. "I don't know why that girl even bothers coming by," Derby would say, his eyes fast and dark and attached to Betsy's face pressed against the window of Pete's retreating car. "They should all be locked up."

Maude became so accustomed to her husband's battering of her family that she stopped listening, stopped trying to assess whether or not she thought he was right. Of course, he was right but only in a bitter, darkened, unearthly sort of way. Besides, she couldn't fault him for having an opinion. His own family incurred the same unquenchable wrath. "My mother should have stayed in Ireland," he'd spit. "She did nobody any good coming all the way across the ocean to make an ass of herself by marrying an American prig with an Irish name. Don't even get me started on my sister," he'd say, his black eyes rumbling with dark thunder. His sister Trini was an entertainer on the Disney Cruise Line. Maude knew he hated that about her. She had only met her once, at their wedding, and she'd seemed nice enough with her dyed black hair, pale skin, and ruby lips. Dead ringer for Snow White. Derby was unhappy that she'd bothered showing up. "I thought you'd died," he said to his sister as she passed by the receiving line after the ceremony. Trini's expression remained pious. "Welcome to the family, Maude," she'd said. It was the only time they ever spoke since Trini left the church and headed directly back out to sea.

An appropriate welcome, Maude always thought, though her wedding day had been relatively pleasant. Lorraine's appendix hadn't yet burst and Pete wouldn't shack up with Mrs. Lindsey for several more years, and they'd gotten in Lorraine's car, driven the hour and a half to Cambridge to find Rutherford, hose him off, and bring him to the church. He didn't give her away because she never belonged to him the way a daughter should belong to her father, but he was there, in the last pew, almost respectable. Maude felt the faint tinge of happiness that he made a return appearance in her life, even though he was later asked to leave the reception because he was begging the other guests for change. Ruth was a no-show at her daughter's wedding because she was panhandling on Hollywood Boulevard and never even knew the event was taking place.

Derby said it was all for the best that her mother had vanished from her life. After all, his mother had always been there and when did that ever help him out? "Never," he said, and he meant it. His mother was barely four feet tall with wispy red hair and bland skin. She almost never spoke, but when she did, her voice often pierced eardrums with its screeching, unyielding, anti-melodic quality. "Good luck with my little bastard," she squealed on Maude's wedding day. "He's a real Irish prig." Derby's father, on the other hand, was a jolly, unpretentious, apologetic man who seemed oblivious to the fact that his entire family thought he was apish and pathetic. "It's grrrreat to call you daughter-in-law," he said with a thick accent. "Can I get you a drrrrink?" Maude stood by stoically while Derby told his father to shut his fat head and lose the fake brogue. "Wha's faaake aboudit?" he said with an over-the-top laugh. Derby had audibly ground his teeth and dragged Maude off to find a cigar for him to smoke.

Later, when Derby was dying of emphysema, he asked her if she remembered what an ass his father had made of himself on their wedding day. "What an Irish prig," he coughed. Maude had been tempted to retort with a cliché the caliber of *takes one to know one* or *the apple doesn't fall far from the tree* or *like father, like son*, but she decided maybe she loved Derby a little and there was no reason to offend him on his deathbed, and it comforted her that he was recalling the day they were married when he was so close to the end. She never really knew where the idea had sprung for him to court her and legally shackle them together, but hearing him talk about their wedding day reminded her that he at least cared enough to remember. "Why do you want to marry that Irish prig?" Pete had said the afternoon she showed up at Lorraine's house with the tiny silver engagement ring on her finger. "Because he's honest," Maude said proudly, but she hid the real reason from everyone. Derby was impotent and asked her to marry him because he knew she didn't want children and seemed incapable of loving anyone, anyway.

Of course, that was only partially true. Derby was definitely impotent, and she thought she might rather not be a mother, but she was wounded by the notion that she couldn't love. Try as she might, though, Maude never did seem to find anyone she loved completely and truly. Except for Austin Reed, before he was recast and dumbed down. She had lived her entire life in Sutherfield Village and never tried to be happy, never tried to find love. It never occurred to her. "Because your parents abandoned you, reckless hippies," Derby would cough. "That's why you're stuck here in this wasteland instead of out in Chicago or New York." Or Boston. He left that one off because of Rutherford, Maude knew it. But she didn't want to be in Boston or any other big city. She never wanted to leave Sutherfield Village. It was the only thing she could rely on, besides her husband. Pigeon Street always intersected with Melville Lane. Doc's Hardware Store always sat a little too close to Curly's, the diner with the worst fries in the county, and Officer Feltmartin could always be found in one or the other, chatting with customers or helping himself to the coffee on the counter. If Maude left Sutherfield Village, she'd leave all that security behind.

"Besides, what good did it ever do your mother or father to go to some big city?" Lorraine asked. None, Maude was willing to admit, but she never wanted to go, anyway. "You should want to go," Derby said. "You should want *something*." Maude took Mud for a walk and thought about what she might want.

She wanted to do what she was doing now: sit on her white leather couch and watch *Days of our Lives* in peace. That'safact Black was king of her living room, master of her world, puppet master of her fate. Betsy had stayed away today; Cork was curled on his mat on the floor. Her grandmother was dead, her father was, too, and so was her husband. So were her in-laws, perhaps even her Snow White sister-in-law, and she presumed the worst was true also of her mother. Her brother was still alive, but he was sure to drool his way to dehydration any minute, and the Special K twins were sure to have their heads bashed together one too many times and then, then, then! Maude would have what she wanted.

Although, she had hoped to stay tuned to life long enough to see if Kevin or Kelvin ever did anything worthwhile in life. One of them was halfway intelligent, although she could never remember which one. They were a homely pair, though, with excessively skinny bodies, oblong heads, and blotchy skin. They shuffled their feet when they walked and had tomato soup breath, and no one really liked them. Maude tolerated them more than she did their older sister Betsy, but she more or less felt sorry for them. "Those Special K nitwits," Derby used to say. "Never even stood a chance, not with those awful names." Maude never said so, but she agreed that Pete had done a terrible disservice calling her nephews by such similar names. "Thought it was cute," her brother had shrugged.

Not that Pete had any idea about what was *cute*. Every year for Halloween, he would dress the twins up in sheets of bubble wrap and Betsy in black garbage bags and explain that they were "useful." Derby stared at him with nothing short of hatred and spit. "*Par*-thetic." Maude dropped licorice into their open paper grocery bags and said nothing. She knew that Pete loved his kids, maybe, and he probably liked Mrs. Lindsay a little. Most days, she was envious of his happiness because she was sure he was happy.

John Black seemed pretty happy, too, especially today since he was lounging on his couch with Doctor Marlena Evans, his formerly demon possessed wife who now served as the town's most accessible psychiatrist. Most days, John had it rough, though, slithering through ventilation systems, fending off shark attacks, hanging out of helicopters, dodging arrows, taking over the world of fashion, commandeering speedboats, escaping fires, going undercover, losing his identity, cursing the DiMeras, regaining his identity, and talking to his teenage daughter about sex. Maude's eyes fluttered, glad she wasn't That'safact Black, even though his life seemed pretty content at the moment.

Then again, so did hers. Her house was small, but today it felt cozy instead of claustrophobic. She looked around and wondered if she should take the opportunity and clean up a little. She was rarely in such a good mood, rarely ready to do anything extra, but something was stirring her. Maybe all the memories. Maybe the shade of happiness shielding her heart.

The shield was a thick one, too. After all, she'd been married to Derby for forty-seven years and she'd learned to protect herself. Before him, she'd never been in love, and even now, a year and a half after his death, she wasn't sure she'd ever really loved her husband. "I was in love when I was young," Lorraine told her before her eighteenth birthday. "But I still ended up here." Maude still remembered the mournful crease in her grandmother's cheeks, the resentful flush in her eyes. "Here," she said again. Now, Maude wondered if she was better off without the soul-crushing fury of love.

But she knew that wasn't true. Derby was right, she had wanted *something* in life, and it wasn't so much love as it was the turgid reality that came along with it. She wanted her bones to pop and groan and splinter with the ecstasy of knowing that she was The Most Important Person in Someone's Life, even if only for a few disintegrating moments. She wanted to taste the underbelly salt of passion. She wanted to be John Black's whore. She wanted to spread her yards of flesh out across the streets and open her mouth.

But she didn't. Wouldn't. Couldn't. She was too old, too fat, too stupid, too content, even though she wasn't the least bit old, fat, stupid, or content. She was small. She was deflated. She was too tired.

Besides, *Days of our Lives* was on.

"When in doubt," Lorraine used to say between drags on her cigarette, "you can count on Salem." And Maude largely agreed. She always knew that the intricate origami birds unfolding themselves on the screen in the form of crummy acting and vapid dialogue lived in the Surreal World that she could understand, if not accept outright. Within the span of an hour, lives changed every day. Loves flourished or severed, families tightened or spread out. Floods, fires, earthquakes, murders, marriages, births, deaths. All the happenings of one hour. Entire lives. Over and done with. Until tomorrow.

Maude regretted how little she lived in each hour of her life. But today, she felt peaceful, and as she closed her eyes in time to the violins signaling the closing credits of the show, she thought about changes she might make after her nap. *Like sands though the hour glass, so are the days of our lives.* But she never woke up.

Written in circa 2002

At Least We've Got Each Other

"Lookit Lester over there," Stacey said, her hand fumbling in the bowl of mixed nuts. "Trying to get straight to third base by pulling that Jew's Harp out of his pocket and playin' some fancy tune."

Morgan gave her sister the stink eye and crunched on a cashew. "Mouth harp," she corrected.

"Whatsa difference?" Stacey asked as she crunched on her own cashew.

"Jewish don't got nothing to do with it," Morgan said. "It's just an ancient instrument."

Stacey sat up a little straighter and gave her sister the hairy eyeball. "Defensive much?" she said. "Whaddayoo care about it?"

Morgan stared into her third of the five whiskeys she'd drink that night. "You know," she said with no inflection.

Stacey paused a moment, sighed, finished her fourth of the seven whiskeys she'd have that night and said, "Anyway, he's gonna try to make it with that girl over there. Pardon me, that *woman* over there. See, he's gonna play that Jew-- *mouth* harp right next to her at the bar. Shameless."

"Who cares," Morgan muttered, scraping her fingers in the nut bowl.

Stacey guffawed. "You do, apparently. If I didn't know better, I'd say you were jealous."

Morgan finished her whiskey and nodded at the bartender. "Joel, hit us up, please," she said in lieu of responding to her sister.

Joel came over and poured generous portions into their existing glasses. "Want more nuts?" he asked.

"Always," Stacey said with a sloppy grin.

Joel smiled back, though more soberly, and said, "Be right back."

"Ain't never gonna happen," Morgan said as he walked away.

"His wife might die," Stacey said with a shrug.

"Maybe," Morgan said.

Stacey was already back on the Lester thing, though. "So you still like Lester," she said.

"Still?" Morgan said.

"You know, after the..." Stacey began.

"Hush your face," Morgan hissed.

Stacey shrugged. "Anyway, *you* know."

"That was one time and it was in a car, for chrissakes, so it barely counts," Morgan said.

"But you liked his mouth harp," Stacey said with an exaggerated wink.

"It's called a *mouth* harp," Morgan said a little too harshly.

"That's what I said," Stacey said.

"Oh," Morgan said.

"So if you like him, go get him," Stacey said too loudly. Lester actually looked over in their direction, so Stacey waved.

"Stop that," Morgan said.

"Seriously, he mouth harped you forever ago and you see him all the time at this stinking bar and you never even talk to him so if I, your very own sister, did not know you still lusted after him, how would he, an extremely dumb man, ever know?" Stacey asked with a little too much logic.

"Here's your nuts," Joel said, placing a fresh bowl between them.

"Thaaaaaanks," Stacey said with an over the top wink. Then she turned back to her sister. "Plus, he's a dude who thinks an ancient instrument will win over girls in bars, so..."

"It's   an   ancient   instrument,"   Morgan   said defensively.

"That's what I said," Stacey said.

"Oh, right," Morgan said. "Well, anyway, he's good at... at... playing it."

Both sisters stopped talking and stared at Lester as he leaned in towards that attractive other woman with his mouth harp.

"I think she's into it," Stacey said conclusively.

"Yeah," Morgan sighed.

"Maybe Joel's wife will die," Stacey sighed.

"Yeah," Morgan said, digging into the new nut bowl.

"At least we've got each other," Stacey said.

"Yeah," Morgan said.

Written in 2013

Guided Hypnosis #32

"Was broken down by the side of the road, yeah
Was crawling in the darkness
like a king snake in the woods
We were hiding in the tall grass, hiding in the tall grass
Just looking for a place to shed our skin
We're gonna summon the Holy Ghost from the battlefield
And in the morning, this old world won't be the same
Won't be the same, Lord..."
~ Widespread Panic

You went into the woods alone. As soon as the cover of trees shielded you from the outside world, you felt the panic in your chest give way to a relief that rushed from head to toe and back again and you already forgot the ones you'd left behind. It was safe here. No one could get to you -- and, even more importantly, you couldn't get to anyone. Oddly, though, the farther you walked into the fortress of trees, the less alone you felt. Your eyes darted backwards time and time again, certain you were being followed by something human -- more human, even, than you. Leave it to you to be haunted by what lives, an undead ghost. Leave it to you to think you could escape from it.

You'd left your car by the side of the road, parked askew, angled into an embankment. You wanted to give it the look of a shipwrecked boat at the bottom of the sea, long forgotten, all its stories washed away. But the truth was the odds of anyone driving by were remote. You'd taken a road less traveled to get here. No one would fantasize about what kind of lives your car once carried. No one would get the chance.

So instead, you imagine driving over that hill and seeing your vehicle, slowing your own and bringing it to a stop. You'd get out and feel the palpable stickiness of the air as you'd call out, "Hello?" to no response. On the ground, you'd see impressions in the grass like someone had been dragged into the woods and you'd stagger back a step. Your cell phone gets no reception here, so you'd be on your own to investigate or not. Even thinking about these things arouses you now as you walk through the woods, your clothing dirty from crawling on your belly through the mud. Upright now, you feel cleansed, renewed. You feel like a new man.

Soon you come to a clearing and everything changes. You hesitate at the edge, frightened that all it takes is the sight of sky above for her voice to fill your head, telling you how you've failed -- her, yourself, everyone. It gets louder when you step back into the sun and you press your hands over your ears which somehow only makes it louder. You stagger to a stop and fall on your knees, your hands pressing next into the ground. Your fingers wrap around blades of grass and you yank them, hard, by the roots. *You are a failure*, she whispers through your mind. Your eyes grow dark as you sit back on your heels, suddenly exhausted. You try to remember the last time you heard her actual voice say anything out loud. It was a long time ago and all she'd said was, "Thanks for the ride," clearly not meaning it as she slammed the door to your now-abandoned car. You'd watched her go into her house and stared hard as she never looked back. You could barely remember what her face looked like, but you would never be able to forget her voice.

She was the one who'd compared you to a snake in the grass, belly down and waiting to attack. She was the one who'd said no matter how many times you shed your skin, you'll still be a predator concealed by tall grass. She was the one who'd said there was evil in you.

As her voice pummels your insides now, you feel more helpless than you've ever felt before. Your head hangs as you try to shout louder in your head to drown her out. But you can't. She's always there. She's the tingle in your spine. You see a shadow dart behind you. You are never alone.

In these moments, you pray. You rock from side to side and you ask for salvation. You clasp your hands to conjure spirits while the trees rustle and call you back undercover.

In these moments you know there never will be an escape, no matter how far you go into the woods alone.

Written in 2015

The Lie That Matters

"Lisa," she lied.

The man didn't laugh so much as he grunted and took a rocking step back. He muttered something no human could understand which she interpreted as, "That's my favorite name." She smiled warmly. It was the least she could do. The man was missing a few teeth and in need of cleansing, this was apparent, but otherwise, he seemed kind. Almost like the sort of guy she'd like, honestly, genuinely, if she wasn't meeting him for the first time on the worst day of her life.

But that, too, was a lie. No, an exaggeration. It was the worst day of her life because she could think of nothing worse than the terrific awfulness of what had happened before she'd dodged down the winded steps of the Copley T station, inbound trains only, away from the badness; but she could think of worse things. She knew they were coming. Worse than this man, covered in heart-tugging black fur that she supposed was hair, she presumed he was a mammal, like she was, this man standing far too close in terms of American social standards, not drunk or stoned or otherwise altered, so far as she could tell, just a man being overly friendly, forcing her to lie once more, but an innocent lie this time. This lie wasn't hurting anyone. This lie was safe.

"I have a donkey and a horse," the man said. He was rolling the palms of his feet to the side, resting his ankles on the ground in a very uncomfortable-looking position. Even the man appeared uncomfortable through his smiles and strange acrobatics. She stared at him for a moment, the same smile she'd offered with her false name still lingering on her plastic face, plastic because she worked in customer service and knew how to smile to the general public. She could pretend this man was her customer at Barnes and Nobles, just a guy who wanted to know where he could find some Flannery O'Connor or books on wicca. She could pretend; she'd had practice. But now, she couldn't even respond to the man, this proximate man whose breath smelled like tomato soup and lemonade, this man with blackened teeth and striking green eyes. She remained motionless, uncertain. The man didn't seem to care. He was asking her where she was from. She wasn't responding. She was thinking about the lie.

She was thinking about the lies that matter. Like, when she was in grade school and her mother told her the bus driver used to be an FBI agent or her elderly babysitter was a personal friend of Stevie Wonder. Those lies, those lies were innocent. They didn't matter. They were spun out of faithfulness, derived from honesty. The faithful, honest attempt of a mother to soothe her overly practical daughter into believing life could be extraordinary. Or when her second boyfriend, a stunning peacock of a boy named Jeremy Winthrop, cool blonde hair, half-lidded blue eyes, faintly stubbled chin, all of nineteen years old, had told her that hadn't forced her to have sex on her parent's couch the day after Thanksgiving the year she turned seventeen, that she'd wanted it, wanted to feel his dick inside of her, wanted to lose the stain of virginity. Then again, maybe that lie wasn't so much derived out of honesty and faithfulness as it was out of a need to believe it was honest or faithful. She could appreciate a good lie for a good cause. She thanked God every day for the good lies.

The man was speaking to her again, but she wasn't listening. By the time she realized he was still focused on her, he was nearly screaming, "LISA!" And she remembered that's who she said she was, thought maybe it might be a good plan to *be* this Lisa for the rest of the day, and fluttered her Lisa-like eyelashes at the man. No, she had never run in a marathon, but, boy, does she find it witty that, while throngs of crazed runners battle up Heartbreak Hill, he will only be running from the bedroom to the kitchen for more beer and Milano cookies, and, yes, she was naturally blonde, and yes, she tried to work out regularly. Being Lisa felt good to her, like she was somehow reborn into innocence, like she was herself again. She wanted to thank the man, but she didn't. It wasn't Lisa's style, so much as it was her own.

As the man told her a story about when he was a boy, growing up in Hell's Kitchen, she slipped back into neutral, plastic grin and all, and her mind drifted back up the stairs, back up to the trouble. There had to be trouble, of course, or else why would she feel such a need to trade places with Lisa, her invention? Yes, there was trouble, of the worst kind. She wondered if Lisa smoked pot; she kind of wanted to, but only if her new alter-ego was cool with it. But then she decided that numbness only prolonged things. The lie was what was at stake for her now. This was a lie that mattered.

"How do you feel about dog racing?" the man asked. She said she thought it was barbaric; that was one thing she and Lisa most definitely agreed on. "How do you feel about lying?" she asked him, and he shuffled back a step. "Well," he said slowly. "Sometimes a rat will eat soup." She stared at him, stared at the narrow spark in his eyes, and heard his howling laughter fill the station, the underground cavern where they waited in vain for the train, where was that train, and he repeated his nonsense response. She told him quite sincerely that she couldn't agree more, folded her arms across her chest, and wondered if he believed her name was Lisa. She wondered if it mattered. She wondered why she'd lied at all, she'd probably never see this man again after today. But she knew why she'd done it -- lies felt good to her today. Better than ever.

She'd had a bad day and this man, this forever-chattering man, wasn't making it any better. She closed her eyes as if that would help, but when she opened them again, he was still there, still standing too close, with his bohemian black hair and his sour breath. She was tired. She needed to get away.

Her boyfriend, for lack of a better term, asked her to leave Boston for the week to travel to New Hampshire with him to visit his brother. She'd said no, sighted work, and didn't answer his calls for three days. He wanted too much from her, had said he loved her too fast, and she was wary of him. As much as she needed a break, as much as she'd wanted to avoid the day she'd just had, a day she knew was coming far in advance, she turned him down because he wasn't a worthy alternative. He was too old for her, taxing almost ten additional years onto her own, and too grounded and too ready for permanence. Also, he was too short. Besides, she wanted nothing permanent. She was looking for Now, not for Ever.

"Amen," the man said, and she wondered if she'd spoken out loud. It didn't matter. She was stuck waiting for the train, the same as he was. It was OK if he knew. It was OK if he didn't. She cocked her head to the side and thought about telling the man the truth.

But she didn't. Instead, she thought about the lie, that terrible lie, that awful lie that had spun her out of her karmic balance and jettisoned her into personal power failure. She also thought about how her feet hurt and how she wished she was speaking to her boyfriend so he could sidle over to her apartment and treat her feet like his own mama. Her mind was drowning in the lie.

At that moment, the train arrived, and the man heaved one last mildewed breath at her as he said, "Stay beautiful, Lisa. It's not easy," and leapt onto the train. But she didn't follow him. She sat on the bench and watched the train pull away, watched her latest lie vanish into the tunnel of darkness on the lips of a man she'd just met.

Written in circa 2003

Animals

Bert said that emus were his favorite kind of animal and I wondered what they were teaching my kid at that school. The asking child was in line ahead of us for the all-tiger carousel at Comerica Park and as she stared at my son with fascinated eyes, I bet a million invisible dollars that if presented with the same question, that Little Miss So-and-so would say "Tigers" and my mind split a step further with one half thinking, "unoriginal, uninspired junior bimbo" and "god, is her mother lucky to have a vanilla cookie child." Her mother was actually staring at me with a mild sense of inquisition as our children chit-chatted and I wondered if maybe there was a bit of pity in those eyes. Made me want to take a nail gun to her forehead, honestly. So what if my kid is an oddball who likes weird-sounding animals better than things like cats or dogs. At least then I wouldn't get stuck with some pet he'd falsely promise to care for before abandoning his post and sticking me with his dirty work. We'd never be able to get the kid an emu, right? It's some kind of bird, isn't it? I didn't even know. I wanted that little brat to ask Bert to explain himself so I wouldn't have to do it. The brat stayed mute, but her mother, well, she took the bait.

"Sweetie, what's an emu?" she asked.

"Why, it's the largest bird in Australia," Bert said, as if every moron knew that, so I rolled my eyes supportively.

"And why do you like them so much?" the mother asked, undaunted.

I waited for Bert to unleash a shit storm of information about heroic deeds this bird had carried out or about how the species assisted with scientific advancements in cancer research or how one emu could destroy an entire pride of lions if it was so inclined. I even let a smug, satisfied grin mug on my face. But you know what that asshole son of mine said?

"I dunno, I think they're cute."

The little girl smiled and even batted her slutty little eyes while her mother clucked her tongue and tilted her head in that "awww, how adorable" kind of way that grownups do with kids. I pursed my lips with sheer annoyance.

"Well, I think that *you're* cute," the mother said as the gate opened, indicating it was finally our turn to board this terrible ride.

"Sit by me!" the little girl said, grabbing Bert by the hand.

The girl's mom and I stood aside as our kids skipped over together to scramble onto side-by-side tigers.

"Your little brother seems like a character," she said with a wink.

I narrowed my eyes as I hiked up my tanktop. "Well, your *granddaughter* seems very average," I said, taking two steps away to watch the carousel spin by without some woman yapping in my ear.

Written in 2013

Guided Hypnosis #24

"Now most days I spend like a child
Who's afraid of ghosts in my mind
I know there's nothing out there
Yet I'm afraid to turn on the lights --"
~ Amos Lee

You never liked being alone so why would you start now? Hunched, drunk, at the table that isn't very stable in your apartment, your balance is off in your chair as you start to lean, your eyes dropping, your mouth sagging, all of your features melting down your chin.

Someone will be over soon.

It doesn't even matter anymore who pings your phone. You answer, unfiltered, agreeing to a hundred things before the sentence can even end and your brain eats it up like sugary snacks -- *nom nom nom -- if you won't make me happy, you can at least keep me distracted.* Your brain has lots of things like this to say.

On the shelf built into the wall, there is a thick layer of dust building a village on books you haven't touched in years, not since you moved here, the place you've been longer than anyone thought you would be. You've forgotten all the titles but your constant stream of visitors will peer at them, giggling, pointing with unfocused intent. There's scientific manuals and young adult novels and mysterious black binders with clear plastic covers. There's a weird collection of toys you've never played with and art you never quite got around to hanging. There's things that make sense and things that don't and you don't pay attention to any of them as much as you take in what attracts and distracts your guest. *Noted*, your brain says meanly with each vapid round of commentary.

On the table that shifts with the slightest nudge, you've got a glass of whisky that was once quite full and is now mostly empty. You lost interest in drinking it awhile ago but you like the comfort of it in your sightline. In the corner is the guitar you play when you are in the mood for sport and on the floor is a record player that has been scratching out some band you once gigged with's vinyl album. You never liked it much, but, then again, you never disliked it either. People would be surprised to learn how little you cared about anything at all. *You're too busy fucking up all the time*, your brain reminds you as you suddenly lean just far enough that the chair slants beneath you and you nearly fall off.

You slowly sit on the floor.

Your back is now resting against the table leg as you reach up to grab the whisky you still won't be drinking and you try to remember the last time you were sober -- the last time you were happy -- either of those things would do. You wonder where your phone is. You wonder when the doorbell will ring. You wonder when you'll feel less alone.

You wince.

Your arms hang heavy beside you as your chin rolls down on your chest. You think your heart's still beating. You think there's still capacity in your lungs. You can't believe how bright it is in here. You can't believe you let things get this far.

Somewhere out there is a woman who would sit here on the floor beside you and hold your hand and help you up. Somewhere out there is a woman who cared, who tried, who wanted more than anything to pour out the rest of the whisky and clear out the cobwebs. But all she accomplished was becoming the snarky voice in your head, shaming you for being you, over and over, relentless, without remorse. Somewhere out there is a woman who held you in her arms and called it *home*; you changed the locks and cast her out and now you can't even remember why, but you blame her still.

Your phone vibrates in your pocket and you draw it out and squint. *Be there in 5* it says. It doesn't even matter who said it. They all turn to ghosts, anyway.

Written in 2015

The Only Shape

It was one of those date ideas that *seemed* like a good idea, but in reality lacked the luster of romanticism he'd hoped for. "I didn't realize it wasn't just going to be us," he said after several minutes of silence had passed between them. She pulled the provided blanket up under her armpits and forced a smile straight ahead. "Yeah, it's cool," she said.

They were sitting in the back row of a three benched horse-drawn carriage that was currently clomping its way through Downtown Cleveland. Sitting snuggled in the row ahead of them was an elderly couple who had their heads bowed together in what he'd imagined was their intimate night out. He wondered how they remained so still and so calm when the front row was occupied by a harried looking young woman with two toddler-aged children who had not stopped demanding snacks and toys since they got in the carriage just ten minutes prior.

"The money goes to St. Jude's," he told his date.

She nodded and stared off to the side. "Worthy cause," she said.

He opened his mouth to say more but closed it just as quickly. It was only his third date with this woman, after all. What did he truly owe her? Their first date had been "drinks after work" when they'd both planned escapes -- he had to get to his weekly basketball game with his bros at the gym and she had dinner plans with her mom -- but when the magic hour they'd both said was their hard out had slipped silently past them like a particles of water in a river, neither of them had acknowledged it until she'd reached over and gently touched his hand. "I really *do* have dinner plans with my mom," she said, almost sheepishly. "Or I'd probably let you walk me home right now." He'd swallowed hard in that moment, wishing his excuse about basketball at the gym was real as well. "Hey, it's no problem. Moms are important. Maybe I'll give mine a call on my way to meet up with the guys," he lied. She'd gotten to her feet, bringing her hand to his face and pulling him towards her. Kissing him once, softly, she'd smiled and said, "Call me, OK?"

He'd sat on the barstool watching her walk away that night and wondered if she meant literally to call her or if it would be OK to text or if he should message her on Tinder where they'd matched in the first place earlier that day. "I will," he said into the thin air of her departure.

Except he didn't. Largely because she beat him to it, calling his phone two days later at nine o'clock at night. "Hey, what's up?" he said, closing himself in the bathroom of a woman who'd invited him up after their first date.

"I got tired of waiting," she said. Did she sound a little buzzed? He couldn't tell.

"Yeah, sorry," he said, his voice getting quieter. "I've been busy."

"What about tomorrow?" she asked. "You busy then?"

"Not really," he said, his mind flashing back to the touch of her lips on his. "You wanna hang out?"

"I mean, I do, but I'm actually not free," she said. "Maybe Thursday? I have that day off. We could do something in the afternoon? I know you said you had a pretty flexible work schedule, so would that work?"

He did some mental math. "Yeah, maybe like three?"

"OK, that works. I'll text you my address. Just come to my apartment," she said before she hung up.

"Sure," he said slowly to the dead line as he gave himself a quick once-over in the mirror before exiting the bathroom and returning to his date-at-hand.

As promised, she texted him around noon on Thursday with her address and he arrived at her door exactly at 3pm with a six-pack of beers she'd mentioned liking. When she opened the door, she flashed a brilliant smile until she noticed the gift he'd brought. "Oh," she said before shaking it off and standing aside to let him in. "Thanks for coming over."

He chewed the inside of his lip. "Yeah, of course. Can I offer you a beer?" he asked.

"Oh, no thanks. I'm on a cleanse," she said airily. "But knock yourself out."

He nodded slowly and looked around. "Your roommate home?" he asked, still standing awkwardly in the door.

"Not right now, but she'll be back from class soon," she said. "You can come all the way in."

"Right," he said. "Sorry."

"Have a seat," she said, gesturing towards a frumpy looking couch.

He sat down and she perched on a chair adjacent to him. "How's your day?" she asked.

He studied her, her long brown hair that had been down on their first meeting was swept up in a messy bun. She wore glasses, something that was different from the other night, and she was in jeans and a tank top instead of her sleek all-black retail work attire.

"My day's good," he said.

"When I called you the other night, were you on a date?" she asked.

"What?" he asked.

"I was just wondering if you were on a date when I called," she repeated.

"No, why do you ask?" He splayed his palms out over his knees.

"You were whispering," she said, her nose scrunching up. "I thought maybe you were trying not to be overheard." She paused. "It's cool if you were on a date," she added. "I was just curious. We did meet on Tinder, after all, so I gotta assume I'm not the only person on your, ya know, dance card."

"I don't really date that much," he said. "What about you?"

She shrugged. "I mostly have the app because my roommate stole my phone, installed it, and created a profile for me."

"Yeah?" he asked, unsure if she was bullshitting him or not.

"Did you think I was inviting you over here for sex?" she asked suddenly.

He felt a wave of panic roll through him. "Why do I feel like I'm about to be on one of those 'gotcha' news shows... Do you have, like hidden cameras or something?"

Her face wore a smile but it lacked warmth. "What a funny conclusion to jump to," she said.

He stared at the beers he'd set on the table in front of him. "You sure you don't want one of these?" he asked.

She shook her head slowly. "No, I'm good. But you go ahead."

He reached over and cracked one open. "Cheers," he muttered.

She laughed. "I feel like I've made things weird. Sorry," she said. "My last boyfriend just lied to me a lot and so I have this annoying thing where I am pretty brutally honest. I've learned that's a turnoff to most men."

He felt better now that a sip of liquid courage had hit his tongue. "Honesty is good," he said.

She nodded. "Let's go for a walk," she said. "I'll get you a thermos to pour your beer into."

He watched her disappear into what he presumed to be the kitchen and re-emerge seconds later with a Planned Parenthood plastic water bottle. Thrusting it in his direction, he accepted it with a "Thanks" and started pouring. At that moment, the door swung open and a tired-looking red head came in with a very heavy-looking bag slung over her shoulder.

"Hi, sorry, I'm not even here," she said as she tried to scoot through.

"This is my roommate Amber," his date said. "She's Wonder Woman."

Amber offered her a rye smile. "I do what I can. Including getting out of your hair."

"We're going for a walk, anyway," his date said.

"OK, have fun!" Amber said as she started to disappear down the hall.

"Help yourself to a beer, if you want," he said.

Amber threw her bag down and nearly lunged towards where he gestured. "I have never needed a beer more, so thank you. You kids enjoy your walk," she said, exiting the room with a flurry of chaotic energy.

"She's great," his date said.

"Seems to be," he said.

"Ready to go?" she asked.

"OK," he said, Planned Parenthood water bottle clutched in his hands.

They left the apartment and walked for almost two hours, just up and down the streets of Cleveland, occasionally hand-in-hand, often with her leaning over to kiss his cheek. Their conversation resumed the effortless pattern it had on their first date, so much so that he forgot about how uncomfortable the date had made him feel at first. When they got hungry, they sought out a happy hour where they both ate and he drank, and he forgot to check his messages -- *that's* how much fun he was having. Eventually, many hours later, she wove her fingers through his and asked, "Wanna walk me home now?" He smiled at her. "Sure," he said.

When they returned back to the place their date had started, things went much smoother, especially since there wasn't much talking. Just an offer of, "Amber works late tonight." He learned quickly how her honesty could translate into very expressive instructions for where he should put his hands on her body, how she wanted to be kissed, and where he could find a condom. "I brought some, too, if you want to save yours," he'd teased, feeling cheeky. "I trust mine, if that's OK," she said, her bra already off. "Yeah, that's fine with me," he said as she turned Iron and Wine on to play through her computer speakers.

Who's seen Jezebel? She was gone before I could say, "Lay here, my love. You're the only shape I'll pray to, Jezebel..."

The sex was good for him -- expert. "Usually girls your age don't have your... sophistication," he said afterwards, turning his head to look at her profile.

She stared at the ceiling. "So you *do* date a lot," was all she said in response.

"Not really," he echoed from before.

She rolled over to lay her head on his chest. "Thanks for a great second date," she said.

For some reason, he knew that what she meant was, *It's time for you to go.* It made him feel uncomfortable somehow -- like this was the opposite of when most dates like this would end. But the heaviness in the air nudged him to count to ten and then ease out from under her.

"I guess I should get going," he said, facing away from her, feet on the ground.

She yawned. "OK," she replied in a neutral voice.

"I'll call you," he said as he put his pants back on.

"OK," she said again before adding a little warmth to, "That would be nice."

He waited until he was down on the street walking towards the bus stop before he pulled out his phone and dialed her number.

"Hi," she said after three rings.

"Hi," he said back.

"Thanks for calling," she said sleepily. "Call me again tomorrow."

Before he could reply, he realized she'd hung up on him. His whole being felt like it was buzzing in the wake of their time together. He'd never felt like *this* before. On the bus, he texted the woman he'd planned to meet up with later that night to cancel and he started to google *romantic dates Cleveland*. That's when he'd seen the horse drawn carriage rides. He remembered how she'd mentioned an aunt who'd taken her horseback riding as a kid. He thought about how she was going to have high expectations for Date Number 3. Right then and there on the bus, he called the phone number listed on the website and left a message on the voicemail. When they called him back the next day, he booked their ride for that night without even checking to see if she was free. His excitement was just that high -- she made him high.

"I have to work. What about Saturday night?" she'd replied when he called to say he had a surprise for her.

"Yes, sure," he said, hanging up to call back and try to re-book.

It must've been in that chaos that he'd missed the fact that they'd be in a carriage built for more than just them. The night was also much colder than it was just two days prior -- such is the schizophrenia of a global warming winter. When he'd picked her up from her apartment and tried to hold her hand on the walk over to meet their carriage, she'd seemed more aloof and distant than he'd hoped. And when he told her what they were going to do, that blank smile he'd seen before returned. "Sounds good," was what she'd said.

Now they were twelve minutes into their carriage ride and one of the toddlers in the front seat was full-on wailing. He watched the elderly couple nestle in and looked over at his date, wondering if she'd get out of the carriage and disappear into the night, never to be seen again.

In his pocket, his phone vibrated with backup plans, when and if that became the case.

Written in 2020

Black and Blue

She held the razor blade close to her pale face, balanced it on the tip of her nose, and stared at the clean strip of metal touching her skin. Her blue eyes were scorching and dry, but she couldn't look away from the smoothness of the blade. She couldn't take her eyes off the neatness of it.

Order.

Mundane life force.

Post-chaos, pre-meltdown.

She tilted her head to the side and moved the razor closer to her eyes. She wanted to smile, wanted to wink at the possibilities, but she'd forgotten how to make her face change from happy to sad. Her eighteen years of teaching herself to be desensitized left her with nothing but an expression of permanent nostalgia. She didn't miss smiling as much as she missed laughing. *Laughter is the best medicine*, her mother used to tell her.

She stared at the razor and disagreed.

She set the blade down on the bed face-up so she could see the shining metal lying beside her on her red and white bedspread. She patted it fondly, as if it were one of her childhood teddy bears, now stuffed under the bed along with every girlish notion she'd ever had. The entire room was stripped clean of any hint of her horribly ordinary, terrifically stale up-bringing. Starting with her bedspread, everything was decorated in bright red and white. The walls, the dresser, the bed, the desk all seemed to scream out against little girl pinks and pastels. Her mother helped her build the rage of red into the room years ago, helped her break through the walls of childhood and build a brighter, more startling cage to hide in.

Picking up a pad of note paper with smiling cherubs, a gift from James, she leaned back against the wall. She closed her eyes and felt her dry lids scrape most mercilessly over her pupils. The pain was temporary, though, and she swallowed it whole. She left her eyes shut as she wondered what to write, what to say, to all of them. To *all* of them. How could she make it right for them all? She couldn't, but she knew she was right, knew she wasn't making a mistake, knew it was her time to step into the light, fade into black and blue.

She opened her eyes without even realizing it and glanced down at her sleeveless arms. She only revealed her bare flesh in the privacy of her bedroom. People got angry and worried when she'd flash her skin in polite company. She hated the stares and the questions and the suggestions of more psychotherapy, of punching pillows or flipping coins, so she hid her arms just like she hid her smiles and her frowns. Hid everything until hiding became more routine than breathing.

She propped the note paper on her bent knees, stared curiously at her naked arms, and felt the reminder of a smile on her dry lips. Her heart began to beat faster as she allowed her fingers to brush slowly over her forearm. Like a graveyard of twisted regrets and missed phone calls and forgotten homework and self-loathing, she fondled the past, fondled the pain of knowing she was at fault, that no one was blameless, that no one deserved to...

Her forearm was littered with jagged edges, poorly healed reminders of how wrong her life was, how wrong *all* life was. Each cut, each blotchy red line, reminded her, *reminded her* that she deserved not to feel. That she had cut away every tumor with her own blade. She didn't need a surgeon, didn't need a professional, didn't need anyone. She didn't even need herself, didn't need her flesh, didn't need this excuse called life to feel so empty and dried up. No, all she needed was a blade to carve out her life, to carve out her purpose, to scoop away her nothingness. She felt the ripple of excitement turn in her stomach as she let her fingers rest on every scar on her arm, some still fresh enough to be covered with a scab.

Dig deeper, dig deeper, next time…

Dig into the foundation of freedom. Dig into the oblivion of black and blue, bruised and beaten, like her arms. Each was swollen and savage-looking from her wrists up to her elbow. She swallowed thickly and wished just one of the cuts would *mean* something, would *make a difference*.

But none of them were deep enough. None of them got to the core of what her life had become to mean.

None of them had killed her yet.

Time to flip a coin? Punch a pillow? Write a poem?

She snatched the note paper off her knees and gripped her pen as she finally knew just what to write.

After scribbling for a moment, she dropped the paper on the bed beside her and grabbed the razor. Without hesitation, she drew the blade swiftly across her wrist until a thin stream of blood spit out of the darkened, nearly black veins. Just as quickly, she drew the blade across her other wrist, this time cutting deeper. Licking her lips with her dry tongue, she slid the blade vertically across each new cut, created her own crossed blossom of tangled blood and flesh. Holding her arms up in front of her face, she watched the blood run down her forearms in slow droplets, an inconsistent stream of startled freedom. She watched the blood drip onto her naked legs without changing her expression. It would take a long time for all of her life to escape through the flaps of skin. She didn't mind. At least her parents wouldn't be around until the next day. She had plenty of time to fade into black and blue.

Lying her arms face-up on the red and white bedspread, she watched the blood trickle onto the clean fabric and stain it. She turned to stare at a book on her shelf and thought about José Arcadio's blood twisting through the streets of Macondo to tell Úrsula that her son had been murdered. Murdered. So had she. And like José Arcadio, her murder would go unsolved. Her mother would hurry up and bury her, quick, grab a shovel.

Dig. Dig deeper. Cover the evidence. Throw dirt on her veins to stop the bleeding.

Her blood would slither under the door and down the steps and out into the park and over a cement bench and up a tree and around a light pole and across a wire and down a fence and into a parlor to stop at the feet of her mother, and her mother would pale, but she wouldn't vomit or become hysterical. It wasn't her family's way. *Punch a pillow, Mother.* Decorum at all times. *Flip a coin, Daddy.*

She lay down sideways on her bed with her arms bleeding up into the false stars of the night and thought about James' bright green eyes before softly closing her own.

* * *

James McGrath shoved his hands deep in his pockets and began whistling as he walked down the dark street. He glanced up at the blanket of stars overhead and grinned at the beauty of night away from the big city. Words aligned in his mind like weary constellations. He was a poet by trade and found there was only so much one could say about the wind in Chicago before he needed a change of venue, a new pallet of experience to help shape his writing. He'd wanted to leave the city to escape the wind, to escape the biting whip of gusting air, to live where there were light breezes and quiet nights.

He liked telling his parents' rich, industrious friends he was a poet because he loved watching their reactions. *"Oh,"* they'd say. *"How lovely."* And then they'd escort their young, impressionable daughters away. He'd wave good-bye to the parents, wink at the daughters, and most of the daughters would make an excuse to find him later so they could sneak out onto the nearest fire escape and look at the stars.

Except the stars were masked by bright lights in Chicago, so James would improvise. *"See Orien's belt?"* Slide hands from face to hips. *"See the Big Dipper?"* Press bodies close together. *"See Cassiopeia?"* Lock eyes, brush lips. *"See how carefully the stars align?"*

He wondered if he should tell people he was an astronomer instead of a poet.

But he had given up the games in the city to find a new way to be, to find value in his life beyond the stars. After twenty years of living under the thumb of his parents, he'd packed himself up and moved himself out. Granted, he was living in his great aunt Angelina's spare room, but it was hundreds of miles away from the awkward, half-caring stare of his parents which was all that mattered. It was the only independent decision he'd made in his life, other than wanting to be a poet. As he walked down the street towards the park, he thought that his new direction was bringing him home, to a new sort of home.

He was on his way to see Annie.

He jumped over the low-swinging chain with the sign reading "Park Closes After Dark" and walked quickly to their bench. It was a cement block with a backrest, but James thought it was the most comfortable chair in existence. He grinned when he saw it and hopped up to perch on top. He scanned the field and didn't see her -- yet.

They had met three months ago, just days after James left Chicago for suburbia. Annie had been sitting on the bench, her short brown hair tucked behind her ears, her legs folded up tightly against her chest. She wore a simple green dress, long-sleeved despite the warmth of early summer, and nothing on her feet. Her skin was pale, and she was unsmiling, with her chin resting on top of her knees. James had slowed as he approached her, captivated by her stillness; she hadn't even blinked.

"Excuse me," he said when he was a few feet away.

She didn't respond.

He got closer. He liked a challenge. "Miss?"

Silence.

Standing right in front of her, he said, "Hi."

Her eyes flicked towards his face, but she was otherwise motionless.

James sat down beside her. "I'm new to the area."

She slowly turned her head towards him. "Good for you," she said.

He grinned. "I'm James," he said.

Her face remained static. "I'm Annie."

He noticed a worn copy of *Big Mama's Funeral* sitting beside her and pulled out the book he had tucked under his arm. Plopping it down onto the bench, he said, "Gabo fan, eh?"

She squinted. "I like magical realism. I've read the *Eréndira* collection, also -- the one with the short stories about the old man with wings and the dead man called Esteban," she said.

He nodded. "You ever read this?" he asked, tapping his own book.

She examined the cover. "*One Hundred Years of Solitude*," she read aloud. She didn't look at him. "No. What's it about?"

"At its most basic it's about a family doomed to end when unto it is born a child with the tail of a pig."

"'Unto it is born'? What are you? A Bible salesmen?"

"Worse -- I'm a poet," he said, brushing his hand through his thick, black hair.

"A poet *is* a Bible salesmen." She frowned and tapped the cover of the Gabriel García Márquez novel. "So does that make this book about the birth of Christ, poet-named-James?" Annie looked at him suspiciously.

James smiled. "It's about a little bit of everything."

They had stayed on that bench for hours that day,

James reading passages aloud from the book, she remaining mostly quiet, listening to him read with her eyes closed. She had finally said she needed to go and, after some persuasion, reluctantly agreed to give him her phone number.

"I'm the weird girl in town," she'd said after writing it in the cover of his book. "Just be warned."

James grinned. "They haven't met *me* yet," he said with a wink.

Annie got up. "I guess they haven't," she said in her retreat.

James smiled now in the early fall night as he remembered that chance encounter so many months ago and fished for a coin from his pocket. Holding a quarter in front of his nose, he squinted and flipped it in the air. Landing with a *ping* on the cold cement of the bench, he leaned over and saw it was tails. He snapped the coin up in his fist and looked across the field to Annie's house. She was later than usual; he could see the light in her bedroom was on. It was the only light in the house.

"Tails says I wait," he said to nobody. "That's always the deal."

After their first meeting were many more, dictated by Annie's melancholy, her decision whether or not to answer the phone when he called. *"Why don't you just pick up?"* he'd asked her once, seated beside her on the bench. *"You know it's me."* She'd looked at him and said, *"My father always flips a coin when he makes decisions, so that's what I do when I hear the phone ring. Heads I answer, tails I don't."* He'd laughed but she didn't flinch. *"Of course I always know it's you, James. But answering the phone is hard, even so."*

He hadn't understood what she'd meant then, nor did he now, but he liked her games, liked her secrecy. He liked her bed, too, liked climbing under the thick blankets with her, even when her mother was home. He liked lying beside her, she looking at the ceiling, never at him; he focused only on her, the tense lines on her face, the true cancer in her thoughts that only he got to see as he lay beside her in her bed. He liked those sun-baked afternoons the best, wasting away the heat of the day in bed with Annie, his best kept secret, even though she wouldn't let him so much as kiss her.

On James' first visit to Annie's house, she'd opened the door and turned immediately up the front staircase in the plain, two-story gray and white colonial to her bedroom. First door on the left. James had stood in the front hallway for a moment, uncertain of whether or not he was invited to join her, and had finally followed her out of sheer curiosity. She was sitting on the floor beside her bed with the thick red and white comforter resting behind her. He leaned in the doorway and tapped his fingers on the white door frame. She didn't look at him.

"Should I have flipped a coin?" he asked.

She shook her head. "Come in. Close the door."

He did as he was told and sat down on the floor beside her.

"You're my only friend," she said, still staring straight ahead. "And I want to tell you something."

"Shoot," he said.

She began to roll up the sleeve on her right arm. "It's my own brand of magical realism," she said.

James peered at the dozen red scabs, some as small as a fingernail, some as long as three inches, on her forearm. She said nothing and slid up her sleeve on her left arm to reveal similar disfiguring marks, one that was barely scabbing. James' heart began to beat faster than he knew it could beat. He leaned in closer to look at the shallow cuts, the cemetery of scar tissue that was her forearms. His eyes widened and his adrenaline pumped through his veins.

"My god, Annie..." he said.

She looked at him, her eyes brightening for a brief moment. "Makes me feel alive," she said.

He looked back at her. "This is the first time in the few weeks we've known each other that I've seen you look almost happy," he said.

She nodded. "It's my secret," she said.

James gently put his arm around her. "Thanks," he said. "For trusting me enough."

They'd spent that afternoon lying under her covers, and she began calling him every time she had a new cut to show him. *"Come quick, James,"* she'd say. *"This one's a little deeper, a little longer. Come and see."* And he'd come, ring the doorbell and be greeted sometimes by Annie, sometimes by her mother. Once, her father was even home. James would scan the falsely content faces of Annie's parents and say nothing. He'd allow himself to be shut behind Annie's door, sucked into her world. Her soft, blue eyes would widen when she saw him, and he would forget that the glamour of his visit would leave permanent bloodstains on his clothes.

"Don't your parents know?" he whispered once into her ear, his head close to hers on her pillow. "Don't they care?"

"They have their own lives," she said. And she sighed. "My mother made me see a therapist once about a year ago. I told him I cut myself because I hated my life, and he said, 'I see, Annie. But couldn't you just hit a pillow instead?'" Annie turned her head so she was nose to nose with James. "I told him I could. That I would just hit a pillow instead, and my mother stopped making me go see him."

James blinked. "Can I kiss you today, Annie?" he asked.

She remained motionless. "No," she said. "Hit a pillow instead." And she'd turned her head back to look at the ceiling.

James would leave Annie and return to his room in his great aunt's house to write poetry about his childhood, about carefree youth, everlasting joy and bliss. He would call his mother in Chicago and tell her he loved her. His mother would respond by asking him how much money she needed to send him. James would tell her, ask her to pass along regards to his father, and hang up the phone. He would stand in front of the mirror in his small bathroom and shave every morning, hold the razor close to his narrow, boyishly handsome face and wonder, as the blade scraped evenly over the surface, if it was worth it to drive the blade deep enough to fold back layers of skin. He thought of Annie's blotchy, black and blue arms and wondered why she *didn't* just hit a pillow. He wondered if she even flipped a coin before turning to her razor.

He was fascinated by her courage.

She'd let him watch her once, watch her cut herself, and he'd felt ill but thrilled at the same time. Real blood looked nothing like it did in the movies. Real blood flowed black out of dark blue veins. She'd let him touch the wound, and he'd shuddered. He'd glowed. Afterwards, she'd asked him why he wanted to be a poet, and he stared at her wound, the blood on his fingers and smiled.

"It makes me feel alive," he said.

James asked his great aunt once about Annie. He knew Angelina knew everyone in town and not in a gossipy, irreverent sort of way. She used to teach at Ridgewood's elementary school and even after her retirement, was never lacking visits from former students and their parents. Of course she knew who her great nephew was spending all his free time with and she never commented about it one way or the other, but James knew she had information for him. So one morning as Angelina worked in her backyard garden, James sat cross-legged on the deck and said, "What happened to Annie?"

His aunt didn't pause in her work. "She just woke up sad one day."

James was surprised by the tone of Angelina's

voice, both caustic and pitying. "What do you mean?"

"She's a lovely girl, Jimmy. I'm glad that you're her friend." She paused to wipe her brow. "But you need to be careful."

James stared at his great aunt's bony elbows, the skeletal hunch of her shoulders. "This town is crazy," he said. "What happened here to make people so... Unfeeling?"

Angelina stopped working and arched her neck to look at him. "What happened to make you so sure that it's this town that's unfeeling?"

James blinked. "I'm sorry, Aunt Angelina. I didn't mean..."

She shook her head and went back to her work. "This is a small town, Jimmy. People here, well, they aren't just people. They're a community. They're a family. And what happens to one member of your family happens to the rest of the family. Annie's sad for her family, for what happened here, but she's much more haunted by it then most."

"What happened?" James asked.

"A boy was killed by a hit and run driver here about five years ago. Never caught the driver."

James waited for his great aunt to go on but when it was clear that she had nothing to add, he pushed, "And..."

"And?" Angelina sighed. "And it affected people."

"Was this boy a friend of Annie's?"

"They probably didn't know each other," Angelina said, her head bowed. "That doesn't matter. She went to his funeral. Everyone did."

James didn't understand and his great aunt, usually so patient and calm, offered no more information than that. So James spent an afternoon in the library reading old newspaper clippings about the boy who died (the librarian knew exactly where to find the microfilms) and wishing he could make the connection between this old tragedy and the one playing out before his eyes. He couldn't find one thing in common.

Now, sitting on the bench, he stared at the bright light glaring from Annie's room and decided he'd waited long enough. He got up, shoved his hands into his pockets, and walked slowly across the field towards her house. He knew she was home alone. Her father was away on a business trip to Chicago, and her mother was at a charity event at the local Red Cross. *"They'll be gone all night,"* Annie had told him over the phone. *"We'll meet in the park as soon as it's dark."*

James grabbed the key from the hiding spot under a pot on the back porch and let himself into the house. "Annie, you here?" he called through the darkness.

No response.

He started up the stairs towards the only light in the house and thought of a conversation he and Annie had in the park a week ago.

"I'm tired, James," she'd said.

He'd closed his eyes. "I know you are, Annie."

"Life is too hard, James."

James got to the top of the stairs and pivoted to the door frame of Annie's room.

"If I decide to die, will you help me?" she'd asked.

James opened his mouth to scream.

"If I decide to end it all, will you give me the courage?" she'd asked.

James felt like he was at the end of a tunnel, dimly light and vibrating. "Nononononononononono....." he moaned.

"If I can't make the cut deep enough, will you do it for me?" she'd asked.

He had smiled and licked his lips. "I'll do whatever you want," he'd said. *"I'll do it for you, if you need me to, if that makes it easier."*

James wanted to run to Annie, his Annie, wanted to pull her away from the pool of blood that swam all around her, wanted to suck the stream of black blood seeping out of the corner of her mouth, wanted to scream at her to open her eyes. *Open your eyes, damn it!* But his feet moved slowly, awkwardly, as if they trudging through four years, eleven months, and two days' worth of rain. "No..." he said again, once, softly. One step at a time, he crossed her plain white floor, freshly stained with her blood, and knelt by her bed, their bed, their special place, and he stared at her face.

She was smiling.

He felt like vomiting.

Breathing faster than he had ever breathed before, he brushed his fingers across her pale cheeks. His eyes traveled quickly down to her arms and saw the gaping holes in her flesh, holes dug by her new razor. She had shown it to him just a few days ago. *"It's little girlish pink,"* she'd said. *"I like pink."* He'd laughed. Laughed. *"Me, too,"* he'd said.

The razor lay beside her body. It was covered with blood. He picked it up and held it close to his face, examined the dirty edges of the blade. His body convulsed as the first fistful of tears bailed from his eyes. He pressed his face against the bloody comforter and clutched the razor in his fist.

"James."

The voice seemed enormous. He turned his head to the side and saw Annie's father silhouetted in the door.

"James," he said again.

James turned his entire body until he was crumpled on the floor beside the bed, still clutching the razor, covered in blood, shell-shocked and sick.

Annie's father stepped into the room. He was a tall man, thick and mean-looking, a polar opposite from James' lanky body and childish face. He stared at James, never took his eye off James, and said nothing.

James let the tears fall down his face, smearing the bloodstains. He pressed his clenched fists over his eyes and tried to breathe.

"James," Annie's father said.

"She's dead," James said. "She's really dead."

Annie's father continued to stare at him. "You're covered in blood," he said after a moment.

James nodded. "There's a lot of blood, sir, everywhere."

He frowned. "Did you call an ambulance? The police?"

"No, I..."

But Annie's father had already picked the cordless phone up off the dresser and was dialing. "Yes, 911, I have an emergency... My daughter..." Annie's father rested his mammoth weight against the door frame, his hand over his eyes. "She's dead, you see. I came home early from a business trip and found her..." Annie's father looked suddenly at James. He narrowed his eyes. "Just send someone," he said before hanging up the phone. Standing with his arms crossed across his chest, he stared at James. "What happened?"

James just continued to cry.

Annie's father moved to stand and look over his daughter's body. He grimaced as he looked at the carnage. "She's smiling," he said after a moment.

James hung his head. "I know."

Annie's father shifted uncomfortably. "She never smiled," he said.

"I know."

Annie's father cleared his throat. "I never liked it that she didn't smile."

James said nothing.

"What's this?" Annie's father asked.

James turned his head and looked up to see him picking up a piece of the cherub note paper he'd given Annie just a few days ago. He watched her father scan the scribbled notations on the page, watched his face darken.

"Is it a suicide note?" James asked finally.

Annie's father glared at him. "You know it's not,"

he said.

James froze. "What is it?"

Annie's father crumpled the note and let it fall on the floor beside James. He picked it up and smoothed it out. Annie had written: *Dear Everybody, I'm tired of feeling nothing. I asked James if he would help end it all for me. He knows how tired I am -- he'll tell you. I write this as he makes the first cut. It doesn't hurt, Mom. It feels good, Daddy. Thank you, James. I'm sorry. Good-bye. Yours, Annie*

James read the note with bulging eyes. "No," he said. He suddenly realized he was still clutching the razor, that his hands were soaked with her blood, that her blood was everywhere on him, that her blood, her conscience, probably ran through his own black veins. "No."

He looked up and saw Annie's father crying. "You killed her," he said.

James stood up, tried to wipe the blood off his face, his hands, his arms. "No."

Annie's father put his hands over his face and moaned through his tears. "She used to smile," he said. "She used to have nice friends. She used to be a normal girl. And you took away her life, her ability to be normal again. Why, James?"

James felt dizzy. "Sir, I didn't..."

"Why, James?" he repeated. "Why'd you agree to help her?"

He felt the bile bubble up in his throat.

"Why'd you kill my daughter?"

James thought of poetry and stars and sex with near-strangers on fire escapes. He thought about the memory of the wind in Chicago, Annie's blue eyes, his own black veins. He thought of stone benches, dirty quarters, pink razors. He thought of happy childhoods, sudden laughter, enveloping arms. He thought of community life, community love, community loss. He thought of time spent under thick red and white comforters, time with a girl he loved but never penetrated, time with a girl more magical than real, time with catastrophe. He looked at Annie, then her father, and said nothing as the sound of police sirens flooded the otherwise windless night.

Written in 2002

Guided Hypnosis #19

You sit alone at a window seat in a small but brightly lit coffee shop near the yoga studio where you just completed practice. You think of the recurring theme during class recapped during *savasana* -- be here now. Seems simple enough until you try to do it but this is one new posture you think you've got the hang of as you walk out of class. Moments ago, a young man with a hurried face brought you the bowl of Greek yogurt you'd ordered, complete with granola and blueberries and three little figs, the house special. A hot cup of coffee, black, is clutched in your hands but you're not that interested in drinking it quite yet. This is a moment for you. This is a moment where time stands still. You smile easily.

But then that moment lurches forward, dragging you with it and your mind starts to color code lists of *things to do: sew button onto sweater, wish Sue a happy birthday, renew the lease on your apartment/look for a new apartment, buy milk.* To mask the smile slipping from your face, you take a sip of your coffee and set it back down. Picking up the spoon, you dig into the yogurt, knowing the contents of this simple bowl will fill you up to the point that you won't think about food again until dinner time.

You think again about the yoga class you just left. You'd never been to this studio before -- it's a little out of your way, but you are feeling like going out of your way for things these days. You'd needed an hour of anonymity on your mat and that's what you got and for that, you feel a deep gratitude. The practice was different from what you were used to but the instructor was clear and direct and you felt your entire being paying attention to what was going on. It's the mantra of the day. It's what you need -- existing in the moment. You try to carry that sensibility with you off the mat but it's harder without the instructor there.

Ordinarily at 10AM on a Wednesday, you'd be at work, sitting at your desk half-heartedly doing your job while streaming *The Diane Rehm Show* on the internet. You are playing hookie today, though. You woke up at 6:45AM, as usual, and you'd even sat up in bed. But then you did what you never did -- you laid back down. You felt a tingle in your fingers. You closed your eyes. You agreed this day would be for you and you went back to sleep. When you woke up at 9AM, you called in sick and you got your yoga mat and you went to class. Diane Rehm would have to forgive your absence today.

As you eat your Greek yogurt, you consider what your global topic of the day would be. *Can't Fix Nuthin'* comes to mind. You think about your average job with an average paycheck in an average office with average advantages. Your mouth slips into a frown again so you put down your spoon and sip at your coffee once more. You ask yourself a series of bold questions in your mind that all simmer down to this:

What do you want?

You sip your coffee again.

A week ago, you sat at your desk, trying to hurry so you could leave and meet some friends in a bar to commiserate about your average existences, when you ran your hand just so over the tops of some file folders and managed to slice a large and menacing papercut into the side of your right index finger. You winced and drew the finger close to your face to examine the division of flesh rapidly filling in with a canyon of blood that popped like a bubble over the rim and traced a red trail before dripping onto your wool maroon skirt. You were surprised to find tears in your eyes and you panicked for a moment about which to wipe away first before your unblemished hand reached for a tissue and dabbed your eyes. It took three more seconds for you to apply pressure to your finger and quiet the bleeding. Wrapping a bandage tightly around your finger, you could feel your heartbeat in the tip of it and it gave you a tingle in your spine. You hadn't felt this way in a very long time.

And now it's a week later and you're playing hookie and you're eating Greek yogurt and your finger is healed. You're trying to exist in this singular moment, like your yoga instructor suggested you should, but it's proving impossible. You *must* consider the past and the future -- these things inform *now*, too, don't they? You sigh and sip your coffee.

When your bowl and cup are empty, you bus them yourself and offer a nod to the friendly staff as you head out the door. The cold hits you hard as you stand on the sidewalk for a moment without moving. You are gripped with the terrifying and liberating realization that you have no idea where to go next. With your hands deep in the pockets of your winter coat and your yoga mat slung across your back like a crossbow, you take in a big inhale and exhale out a fog and you let gravity or intuition or the grace of god move your feet down the road.

Written in 2013

Wildflowers

He held this image in his head that would come to him in unexpected moments. It was his daughter when she was six or seven years old, hand extended with a small bunch of daisies clutched in her fingers, her fist so tiny and deadlocked around the necks of those wildflowers. He could see, so vividly, the bright yellow centers, the sturdy white petals, the bowed heads that come along with being so cruelly uprooted. He could see the startling green of the grass beneath her feet, the soft pink of her hooded sweatshirt, but he couldn't see her face. He could never see her face. Only the flowers. Only they were clear. He didn't know why, he didn't know why.

He hadn't seen his daughter in seven years. She'd be a full-fledged teenager by now. He wondered if she ever thought about that moment she'd thrust those daisies at her old man. He wondered if the memory was even real at all.

Then he'd reach for another beer.

He understood why she'd been taken away from him, but, even so, he missed her. He wished he knew her, even just a little. He wished he had more to go on than a fist full of flowers and a fuzzy face. Lily Ann. His daughter, Lily Ann.

She lived in Albuquerque, New Mexico with her mother Sandra. Last he'd heard, Sandra had gotten married again, but who knows what that guy was like. He hoped he was good to his daughter. He hoped she was loved and being educated about life and called the guy *dad*. Lily Ann deserved a dad, after all.

He'd screwed up the chance. He'd been there to hold her when she was born and he'd helped feed her and bathe her and change her diaper when she was a baby. Things had been different then, things had been good. His work was steady and he and Sandra had a good thing going in Albuquerque. Lily Ann made things even better. He loved telling people, "She's my daughter." He loved holding her up and showing her off and even the soft satisfaction he'd get when he'd generously hand her over to someone else to cuddle her but she'd reach back for him. "It's OK," he'd coo, his heart so full from being needed by her.

But he'd never been good at merging sex with love, so things with Sandra never went smoothly. She resented his bond with Lily Ann, since she went to work and he stayed home with their baby. She'd glower every time their daughter toddled towards him instead of her and he knew it was a matter of time before it would escalate into one of their all out brawls.

When Lily Ann was three, one of those brawls landed Sandra in the ER. He'd had to drive her there after he shoved her and she fell back and hit her head on the edge of the counter. Some of the blood had gotten on Lily Ann's clothing. He was court ordered to stay away.

But he didn't give up -- he didn't let what complicated his life with Sandra interrupt his connection with his daughter -- so he got a lawyer. He took all the necessary legal steps. He was allowed to visit his daughter again. Sandra got over hating him and even let him move back in.

In the year and a half that he'd been waiting for this moment, though, he'd crashed on a lot of couches and learned to cope by drinking heavily. It was easy when that's what his friends offered him as a condolence for being handed a restraining order and no visitation rights to see his own child. He didn't know this kind of pain was possible -- this pain that screamed through the roots of his very being, feeding into his impulses and his mindset and his self-worth. All he wanted was to be with his daughter. He searched for her in the bottom of bottles of beer -- and then whiskey -- and then started swallowing any substance he was handed that promised to shutter the pain. By the time he returned to live with Sandra, his brain had been changed. Maybe too much.

Lily Ann was four and a half and she'd cling to her mother when he came near. "Baby, don't you know me?" he'd ask, gently reaching out towards her. Sandra would pat their daughter on the head and say, "Give her a minute, OK?" He'd look at her and swallow resentment.

As time went on, though, they got back into the swing of their old life with him taking care of Lily Ann and Sandra going to work. The balance of power shifted back to familiar grooves, except that now he was quietly getting drunk or high before taking Lily Ann to the park or to music class or to preschool. He'd sit outside, his eyes puffy, his skin bloated, and he'd try not to get sick in public. He'd feel on edge, like the other parents *knew,* so he was ready, so ready, to fight back, to yell, "She's *my* daughter and you have no rights!" He'd take Lily Ann by the hand and he'd walk her home, slowly, so slowly, his heart percolating with the observation of her new discoveries. It was renewal to see her awe and wonder at the simplest thing.

Like a fistful of daisies thrust in his direction.

By the time that moment happened, he was getting publicly drunk every day. He never put Lily Ann in the car when he was like that, so he didn't see the harm of harnessing a solid buzz. It numbed the ferocious beating of his heart that he might lose his daughter again -- things never really got better with Sandra. He spent a year or more sleeping on the couch while she came home late, never hiding the fact that she was out with other men. One of those nights, he waited up for her, but not on the couch -- in *her* bed. Lily Ann was sleeping across the hall while he sat with venomous thoughts coursing through his body. *How dare she diminish me in this way*, his brain seethed. He waited in her bed until she got home and when she flipped on the light and saw him blackout drunk, she tried to yank him by the shoulder which toppled him to the floor. He lay there, unmoving, a small pool of drool collecting by his turned head, and she panicked. "What have you done?" she muttered, certain he had overdosed. She called the paramedics, which woke Lily Ann up. He didn't remember much about that night except that his daughter had cried. He remembered her cry.

Sandra called him an *unfit father* and produced a year's worth of documentation about his drinking and drug use and physical abuse towards her. His heart burst. "I'm an unfit boyfriend," he conceded in a deposition. "But I love my daughter."

The courts sided with Sandra.

He lost his daughter.

He moved out of Albuquerque.

He reached for a beer.

He thought, maybe, over time, Sandra would relent, like she had before, but she renewed her restraining order against him annually, like clockwork. It crushed him to think about what his daughter was being told about him. It crushed him to think Sandra might not ever talk about him at all.

Over the years, he bounced around a few different places, never lingering too long, living mostly in his car, except for when he could land somewhere for a bit where an old Army buddy had space for him. Eventually, he landed in Altoona, Florida when an uncle left him his trailer home in his will. He settled in there, he kept to himself. When folks asked about him, he told them about his time in the Army and that usually distracted them from asking much else. Every night, he'd lay in his narrow bed, stare at the ceiling, and try to remember what his daughter's face looked like.

One morning, early, seven a.m., there was a rattled knock at his door. His stomach felt queasy, his brain saturated, his limbs hungover, but he still dragged himself to answer.

"She's been sitting here for awhile now, be responsible and let her in."

It was the little old lady who lived next door. Mrs. Mabel. He didn't even know if Mabel was her true last name or if it was her first name with a *missus* tacked in front. She'd been by with food for him from time to time and stopped to chat with him on the rare occasions he'd sat outside with a beer. He certainly had no idea what she was talking about at that moment.

Then he looked down.

Two big, brown eyes looked back up.

They were attached to a smooth, brown-furred face in a thoughtful head tilt, two triangular ears spiking upwards, all attached to a small but muscular body, complete with a long, wagging tail.

"She ain't mine," he said, as the dog scampered past him into the trailer.

Mrs. Mabel chuckled. "Better tell her, then," she said, spinning on her heels and heading back home.

He stood there a moment longer, trying to process what had just happened, before turning around to see the dog had hopped up on the lounger and was looking at him expectantly.

"Hi," he said.

The dog wagged her tail.

He cleared his throat and stared at her. She wore no collar. He didn't know what to do. "Um, let me get you some water," he said.

He stepped into the kitchenette and pulled a plastic tupperware container to fill. Setting that on the ground, he next reached into his refrigerator to pull out what was left of his lo mein, which he dumped into a second tupperware container. "Here," he said.

The dog jumped off the lounger and descended on the offerings while he hung back and wondered what to do after breakfast was served. He moved over and sat on the lounger, feeling dazed. When the dog had enjoyed her fill, she trotted back over and hopped up beside him. Setting her chin on his lap and staring up straight into his eyes, he felt a surge of belonging that he hadn't experienced in more years than he cared to admit.

"Hi," he said again.

He and the dog sat there through the full rising of the sun, well into morning, and he talked. He talked and talked and talked. He told the dog about Lily Ann and Sandra. He told her about being in the Army and how that had helped him stay afloat in these last few years by having that buy in. He told her about how he'd never been good at being a boyfriend, how easy it had been for him not only to lay a hand against Sandra, but against other girlfriends before her, because that's what he'd seen his father and grandfather do -- but how he'd never, never hurt his daughter. Then his eyes would trail to the sink of empty beer bottles and he'd rub his face and look seriously at the dog. "I mean, I never *hit* Lily Ann. I never hurt her like that." The dog remained content through this dialogue, happy to have him scratching her ears and rubbing her belly. He was in the middle of telling her about his latest plan to try to get a message through to Lily Ann when the dog hopped off the lounger and went to stand expectantly by the door.

"Oh," he said. "Yes, of course."

He got to his feet and walked to the door and hesitated with his hand on the knob. "If you don't come back, I understand," he said at last, swinging it open.

The dog scampered outside, peeing right at the bottom of the steps.

"You claiming me?" he chuckled.

She took a few steps and then looked back at him, as if to say *c'mon*. He slid his feet into some flip flops and did as he was told. She darted out ahead of him, but didn't go very far. As they walked along, he grabbed a handful of trailer park provided poop bags, an initiative started by some do-gooder residents, ready to do the responsible thing when the time came. Which it did.

"Maybe I should get you something to eat other than leftover Chinese food," he muttered as he cleaned up after her.

As they walked around the trailer park, he kept expecting someone to call out, "Hey, girl, there you are, come on home!" But no one did. A few folks said, "Did you get a dog?" or "What's her name?"

"Daisy," he said.

The next three weeks settled into a routine: he got some proper dog food and a squeaky toy that looked like a pig. He bought a collar with a tag that said *Daisy* and his phone number. He hung a leash by the door, though he never used it when they would go out for their long walks together. Daisy had boundless energy and teased him into playing. They would walk to the lake and she'd insist they walk around it, not just sit on the edge and watch the water lap against the shore. If the morning was hot, he'd throw a tennis ball in and she'd swim out to reclaim it. But mostly, they'd walk together and talk.

He started to notice the accumulation of beer bottles in his sink lessened. His head was clearer. His body felt alive. The cage around his heart demanded to have its key unearthed. At night, he'd lay in bed with Daisy's head on his chest and as he'd lay a calming palm on her back, he'd try and try and try to remove the static from the memory of Lily Ann's face.

He couldn't, though, no matter how hard he tried. Daisy would lick the tears from his face when his frustration made him cry.

On the first morning of the fourth week, he was up early to take Daisy for a walk when he saw Mrs. Mabel sitting in the chair outside of her trailer.

"Hey," he said, probably initiating conversation with her for the first time since they'd become neighbors.

"Good morning, John," she said. "Good morning, Daisy," she added, reaching down to pat the dog's head.

"I wanted to say thank you," he said.

"What for?" Mrs. Mabel asked.

"For Daisy," he said. "If it wasn't for you, she'd've never been mine."

Mrs. Mabel smiled softly. "You'd've seen her when you opened your door. I didn't do much besides let you know she was out there."

He laughed. "Even so, thank you."

"I'll simply say you're welcome," Mrs. Mabel said.

He turned to continue on his way, but then paused. "Where do you think she came from?" he asked.

Mrs. Mabel leaned back in her chair. "We don't choose who comes into our lives. Especially god's creatures, like Daisy. She chose you, I'd reckon," she said.

He blinked. "No one's ever really done that before," he said.

"Your daughter did," Mrs. Mabel said. "Lily Ann?"

He froze. "What did you just say?"

"You told me about her once," Mrs. Mabel said. "Said she was your whole world." She paused. "I'd never seen a man so heartbroken than when you told me about her."

He swallowed hard. "I didn't know I'd done that. Told you about her."

Mrs. Mabel nodded. "You'd seemed... out of sorts," she offered politely. "I told you then that your daughter knew you loved her and then you'd gone back inside."

"Right," he said. "I'm sorry if I was rude to you that night."

"Oh, no, you were fine," Mrs. Mabel said. "Sad... But fine. Now that I think of it, it was only about a week before Daisy showed up on your doorstep that we'd had that talk."

He looked down at Daisy who was sitting at his feet. "Well, anyway... Thanks," he said.

"Yes, of course," Mrs. Mabel said to his back as he prompted Daisy to follow him.

They walked their usual route down to the lake, the sun shaking off the inkiness of night to reveal warm oranges and pinks and purples in the sky above. He sat down by the water, which wasn't his usual move. Daisy looked back at him with her head at a tilt.

"Come sit here," he said, tapping the ground beside him.

But instead, Daisy sat down right where she was, a cluster of wildflowers right at her feet.

Written in 2020

Grandpa

He was the kind of old where the only name anyone called him anymore was "Grandpa." Even his mailman, even his dentist, even his next-door-neighbor, who was the kid brother of his best pal growing up. "You're only four years younger than me, Lucas," Grandpa would grumble. Lucas would shrug merrily and say, "But what an important four years." Grandpa couldn't argue with that.

He lived alone in an apartment on 5th Street. He'd lived in this very same apartment as a bachelor back before he'd been shipped off to war and then returned without scars to marry, at the insistence of his own fear-inspiring mother, a holy terror of a woman named Bea. Bea commanded they live in a blue house with a white picket fence to guard their property line and get a beagle to stand guard when they weren't home. Their four children Rachel, Anthony, Jessica, and Peter Junior spent their formative years spiraling upwards into adulthood at that house and Bea stood proudly in the driveway with a rolling pin dusted in flour and smiled with determination at the success of her family compound. Grandpa, who went by Peter Senior in those days, cowered by his wife and children and dog on his way in and out of the house each day, finding that he'd grow a little taller in stature (or, rather, losing his slouch) as each of those dreaded family members moved away or, in the case of his wife, died. Bea, of course, was the last to go, hanging around long enough to see each of her children marry at least once and bear an offspring. And then, as if she'd accomplished everything she needed in life, she laid down with a great sigh and didn't rise up again. Grandpa, who was already steady on the path to assuming that as his full-time name, felt nothing but blissful relief when his wife died, immediately putting the house up for sale and puttering back over to 5th Street to see if there were any units available for rent.

Now what he did with his time was ignore phone calls from his Type-A children and watch infomercials about cleaning products late at night when he couldn't sleep, which was almost daily. "How can a mop head be so mesmerizing?" he'd say out loud to thin air. Then one night after a particularly grumpy day that ended with supper next door with the ever-antagonizing Lucas ("Grandpa, let's form a shuffleboard league! You can be our team captain!"), Grandpa slipped into bed and found sleep easily. It was only when he had a dream where Bea was standing over him, watching him get some solid sack time, and still barking orders at him as he slept in his subconscious that he awoke and rubbed his weary eyes. Flipping on his old boxy television set, he nearly fell out of bed as the image on the screen of a buxom blonde with bright red lips was seductively saying, "Call me, baby. First three minutes are free." And then a long string of numbers flashed on the screen. Grandpa blinked and, without thinking, grabbed his bedside phone. Dialing quickly before the numbers could go away, an automated voice answered, asking the caller, in this case Grandpa, if he was at least eighteen years old. And did he need this repeated in Spanish? Grandpa swallowed hard and nearly hung up but the buxom blonde was still on his television screen so he clung to the phone for dear life and admitted he was well over the age of eighteen and English was just fine, thanks. Moments later, a sultry voice filled his ear.

"Hey, baby," it purred.

It had been so long since anyone called him anything but Grandpa, he very nearly popped with exuberance. "Well, yes, hello," he said, trying not to sound like the retirement age beast that he was.

"What can I... *do* for you?" the voice continued.

Grandpa paused. "Are you the lady from the infomercial?" he asked, his mouth dry.

"I'm whoever you want me to be, baby. What's your name?" the voice hummed.

Again, Grandpa paused. "Well, I..." He tried to form the word "Peter" in his mouth but it all gummed together. "What's your name?" he asked instead of answering.

"Whatever you want it to be, baby. What do you want it to be?" the voice asked.

Grandpa paused and thought long and hard about this. There had been another woman during the war, a pretty nurse he'd met in a hospital in France when he'd gone to visit an injured buddy. He'd kissed her once and she'd smiled sadly at him and admitted she was in love with someone else back home and they'd parted like they'd started: star-crossed. Her name was Isabel.

"Isabel?" he'd squeaked in a voice unlike his own.

"Oooh, Isabel, yeah, baby, I like the way you say my name."

Grandpa hadn't held an erection in more years than he'd care to admit and he didn't now, either, but he felt the old strain of *try* in that moment. "Why, thank you," he mustered.

"What are you wearing, baby?" the voice persisted.

Grandpa looked down at his worn out pajama set. "Pajamas," he said.

"Oooh, I bet they look good on you," the voice said. "Want to know what I'm wearing?"

"Sure," Grandpa said, his voice still a bit pitchy.

"*Nothing*," the voice confessed. "Your Isabel is stretched out naked on the bed. Maybe you should take your jammies off and then we could be naked together."

Grandpa felt a lump form in his throat. "Well, I..."

"Here, I'll help you," the voice purred. "Pretend my hands are your hands and feel my fingers undo the buttons on your top..."

"Well, how did you know there were buttons, Isabel?" Grandpa asked, surprised both at the question and his willingness to call this stranger *Isabel*.

"Because I can *see* you. I'm your Isabel, aren't I?" the voice asked.

Grandpa realized he was nodding and made himself stop. "OK, I'm unbuttoning my pajama top..."

"No, silly. *I* am," the voice corrected.

"Oh, right, yes, well," Grandpa said.

"OK, now, slide the top off and drop it on the floor."

"OK," Grandpa said.

"Now feel my hands slide up and down your legs. Let my hands come to rest on your waist and my fingers slowly, so slowly, pull your pants down and toss them to the floor as well."

Grandpa did as he was told, something ingrained in his brain after forty-some grueling married years to Bea, a different sort of dominatrix than this fictional Isabel but a dominatrix nonetheless.

"OK," he said when it was done.

"Oooh, isn't this better now?" the voice asked.

"I've got boxers on," Grandpa confessed.

"Well, take them off, silly," the voice teased.

Grandpa did as he was told. "OK, so..." he said.

"Now we can really get things going," the voice said, a sense of urgency entering her voice. "I'm going to start by..."

And then an automated voice cut in, asking for Grandpa's credit card information to continue, reminding him it would cost fifty dollars for the next hour (a flat fee, even if he hung up before the hour was up) and an additional two-dollars-per-minute after that. He considered it strongly for a minute and then reluctantly hung up the phone. Looking down at his limp and non vigorous body there was no way he'd get his money's full worth with this, but the flush of potential that had filled his body left him restless all the same. Lying there, naked, with a new infomercial about a workout ball now on the television, he thought about the real Isabel and how happy his life could have been with her by his side instead of the tyrannical Bea. He imagined his four children Patricia, Karen, Jesse, and Otto and their springer spaniel living in a pleasant yellow house without a fence around it and his wife Isabel swinging happily with him on their bench porch swing. The unrestricted joy of this fantasy filled his entire being until it tingled and when he finally opened his eyes he was quite shocked to see the full extent of how in love with this dream his naked body truly was.

"Well, I..." he said, his eyes popping.

It took a few joyous minutes to regain his regular equilibrium and slip snuggly into his pajamas and back under his covers but he slept like the *baby* his pretend Isabel had termed him and woke up the next morning a brand new man who stuck out his hand to people both known and unknown and said, "From now on, you can call me Peter," even his grandkids, for he was born again, knowing that simply imagining possibilities could be the meaning of a life well lived.

Written in 2013

Guided Hypnosis #21

Wisdom comes from sorrow and grief
All of the seasons, honey, the trials and treasons
why can't you see it's just you and me?
We're on the same side.

Buffalo Clover, "Same Side"

You stare at the deli menu and wonder if anyone ever orders the headcheese. After you leave here with the sandwich of your choosing, you'll be meeting up with a friend who's vegan. You imagine her face wrinkling up at the thought of gelatinous pig remnants being consumed in her presence and wonder if maybe today *you* will be the one to place such an order. There are still three people in line ahead of you. You have some time to decide how worth it that choice might be.

While you wait, your eyes drift to the television above the condiment station and your lips stay pressed in a flat line while you stare at the muted fans at a European-style football game trumpeting through vuvuzelas in support of their team. You think of a know-it-all friend on Facebook who recently posted an article about how those plastic horns spread cold and flu germs "more rapidly than coughing or shouting," thus making them a biohazard in those overwhelming crowds of *soccer* fans (as this friend so Americanly put it). Your flat lips form a curved line imagining the apocalyptic end of humanity beginning from such an innocent if not patriotic action.

But you are soon returned to the immediacy of the moment when a song by a new-to-you band comes through your earbuds and you listen with unexpected gravity to the lyrics. You wonder: does wisdom only come from sorrow and grief? You wonder: is it just you and me? You wonder: are we on the same side? Your lips flatline again as you answer each question with the same word: yes. This revelation doesn't bring you any joy or sense of satisfaction.

What it does bring you is to the front of the line where you remove your earbuds and, with your eyes on the headcheese, you order the honey roasted turkey and then you stand aside, waiting for what you've asked for to be handed to you so you can leave this depressing place and push out into the sunshine where your vegan friend who has not just played in your head will smile pleasantly and talk to you for hours about the weather report. You will smile pleasantly, too, as if you practiced, as if your goal is not to spread the disease in your head to others, as you commit those lyrics to memory only to forget them right away.

Written in 2013

Love Letters Make Good Foreplay

For absolutely no reason, she sat down to write a suicide note. She wasn't really suicidal, to be clear, but she was thinking about dying.

She was thinking about a man with a mustache who sometimes came to collect her rent check. He was probably related to her landlord, perhaps cousins, but she never found it necessary to ask. She assumed they must be related because they had the same chunky nose, the same wide mouth, the same fat hands, but the man with the mustache had something that the landlord lacked, something that told her with almost stone-cold certainty that the two men didn't share the same parents: the man with the mustache had distinctly flat gray eyes, void of vulnerability which also made them humorless and intensely wise.

Her landlord called her Ladybird because she decorated her door with a small wreath complete with a fake bluebird and he had an overwhelmingly boisterous laugh. He came at eight a.m. sharp on the first of every month to collect the rent because he bothered to know she left for work at 8:10 and he always brought her an apple cinnamon scone. The man with the mustache never spoke to her more than was absolutely necessary and he always called her by the name that appeared on her lease – both first and last – and never appeared at her door until late afternoon. He always smelled of whiskey and sometimes pot, appeared in need of a shave and a shower, and she loved him.

She never knew when he'd be making an appearance and sometimes long stretches, even up to a year, would go by without him knocking on her door. She was patient, though, and grew to anticipate the first of every month like some kind of rare lottery that only she got to play. Scratch and win. Pick some numbers.

She was thirty-three years old and she'd lived in her

Dayton, Ohio apartment for seven consecutive trips around the zodiac. She worked in a bank but wished she read tarot cards like her mother had before she drowned in the bathtub. The uncle who raised her used to say her mother did it on purpose, sucked that water right into her lungs, and that she was the reason her mother did it. He used to say this from outside of the shed door where he locked her when she got crumbs around the toaster and then he would read her passages from The Bible. Also, she played the trombone, loved cats but couldn't commit to owning one, and she went to college in Virginia for art history.

When she was young and in school, she'd been shy, but she was shy in such a way that she intrigued people. She had lots of friends, a few lovers, the occasional brainwashed recruiter of one kind or the other. She learned early on that if she stood quietly in the midst of chaos, she became a magnet for those either seeking peace or wishing to instill peace in others. This was the most important thing she ever learned about herself and when she left school and served a brief stint as an accountant's housewife, she decided what was most important for her was to learn how to center that peace in herself.

Her ex-husband told her once that she was like a tiny, fragile, kaleidoscopic bubble that was always about to pop. He was always trying to get her to cut her hair short and go to therapy. He loved her too much and she knew it and she asked him for the divorce. He blamed the decision on her uncle for locking her in a dark shed when she left crumbs around the toaster and her mother for falling asleep in the bathtub. She'd simply asked him to sign the papers and she'd moved from the tiny college town in Virginia to the Ohio city where her mother said her father, whom she never met, once lived.

Not many people knew her in Dayton and while she got along with her coworkers, she wasn't friends with any of them. She didn't enjoy reality TV or shop at Victoria's

Secrets and loud bars lost their appeal once she graduated from college. She did enjoy roller skating (oh, the lost art!), had a guilty obsession for children's films, owned every Carole King album, and she was obsessed with tarot cards, even though she never was very good at reading them. She still owned her mother's deck, the one thing of hers that she smuggled securely to her uncle's. Those cards were sacred to her, so much so that no one, including her ex, knew she still owned them. She knew that all the tiny quirks that once attracted people to her, even the invisible ones, were now tiny albatrosses around the neck; people were wary of her.

Except for the landlord who thought she was charming and intricate and lovely. She had overheard him telling his wife that very thing once shortly after she renewed her lease for the first time. This both pleased and puzzled her and it was three months into the second year on her lease that the landlord did not knock on her door at eight a.m. on the first of the month, but, instead, a man with a mustache and flat, gray eyes rapped his knuckle against her door at 5:37 p.m., only seven minutes after she'd returned home. He was there for the rent, he said. He'd called her by the name on her lease – both first and last. He was carrying a zippered bank envelope and a list of all the tenants. She'd handed him her check, he'd thanked her, crossed her name off the list, and moved on to the next apartment.

She loved him immediately, without warning.

So when she sat down many moons later to write a suicide note on plain white paper, she wrote it to him.

It began: *I love you, stranger.*

But she crossed that out and wrote: *Even though you're a stranger, I love you, I love you so much I am choosing to die for you.*

That was crazy.

She crumpled the paper and started over on another sheet of plain white paper.

I love your mustache and your gray eyes. I love when you collect my rent check. All day, on those days, I anticipate coming home and awaiting your knock. Many times, I've thought about answering the door naked.

She paused and added, *or maybe taking my clothes off in front of you.*

She read the note aloud and felt a blush rise in her cheeks. Quickly, she put the note down and began to pace. What if she gave the note to him the next time he came to collect her rent? What if she merely did what she wrote and shredded the scripted plot?

She didn't want to think about it more, so she sat back down and wrote: *I do believe I will be forced to take drastic measures against myself if you don't want to see me naked and you don't look forward to seeing me again. What those drastic measures might be, I cannot say, but if you find me drowned in my bathtub, please show this note to no one and know I put myself out of my misery because I made myself miserable. Let them say I am my mother's daughter. You will know I'm actually your foolish admirer.*

After reading the entire thing once more aloud and affixing her signature, she put it in a plain white envelope and tucked it in the box with her mother's tarot cards.

Even though she almost forgot the letter existed, there was something different about her after she wrote it. She was still quiet and shy, she still worked at the bank and almost never even touched the tarot cards, but there was a subtle confidence in her that never existed before. She wondered if even her ex would notice she was less of a tiny bubble about to pop. Just this notion that she could end her own life if her advances towards love were rejected gave her an enormous sense of control over everything around her. Her life was her own; her peace centered.

Then the day came when her landlord did not knock on her door at eight a.m. It was spring, but the day was overcast and cold. From the moment she sat down at her desk until her shift ended, her palms were cold and clammy. A client even recoiled when they shook hands and stammered an embarrassed confession that her touch "gave her the shivers."

She thought about coming home from school and finding her mother dead in the bathtub, an empty glass of wine on her naked torso, her face bloated and peaceful, and how she hadn't been afraid or repulsed but had grabbed hold of her mother's hand and pressed it against her own face and hadn't moved until the phone rang and she had to tell the caller why her mother wasn't available to talk.

She survived that day, though, and so she survived this day at the bank. Brimming with anticipation about when the man with the mustache would arrive, she headed home at her usual time. But when she arrived, her door was unlocked and the man with the mustache was sitting on her couch. She stood in the doorway and stared at his profile, grisled and serious, and wondered if it was love or fear raising her heart rate.

He turned and faced her and greeted her by the name on her lease – first and last – and then he said something remarkable. He said: *I had a dream that you drowned in the bathtub because of love.* She didn't react visibly, so he continued: *You looked beautiful, even dead.*

She shook herself free from her trance and moved in front of him. She asked him what he was doing in her apartment without her permission. He offered a passive shrug and admitted he thought maybe his dream had been true, it was so real. She studied his face, amazed by its intensity, and asked what he would have done if he'd found her dead.

He looked her directly in the eye and said: *I'd have stayed with you.*

She sat down on the couch beside him and wrapped her fingers around his. She said, *But you came and saw I wasn't here, yet you stayed.*

He cleared his throat: *Yes.*

She asked why and he simply shook his head. He said, *The dream was peaceful, just like it is here right now.*

They sat together in silence until the apartment became completely dark.

Written in circa 2007

None of This is the Present

"You don't like beaches," she said. "That's the reason this will never work out."

He smiled wanly and forced a laugh. "Yeah," he said. "Yeah."

She brushed her fingers across his forehead, pushing a stray strand of hair out of his eyes and thought about how many times she'd used that line after half a lifetime together. It was true and false all in the same instant and she chose to think about those sorts of trivial generalities now that he was lying in a hospice bed, waiting for the stomach cancer to win.

Before she sat down to write this story, she had considered giving him something else, another kind of terminal disease, had leaned heavily on the car accident possibility but her own sixth sense told her that she was going to be killed someday in a car accident and she didn't want that irony to be reflected on her telling of his passing. Instead she waffled back and forth between *some kind* of cancer and *some kind* of illness caused from years of hard living, something like emphysema or clotted arteries. She gave him cancer because it was the disease she was meant to die from but wouldn't. Just like he was the man she was meant to avoid but wouldn't.

His name was Paul or John or Richard or George, a generic man-name, not important. She thought about literary students puzzling over the post-reading quiz, the *Who are the characters in the story?* question and not remembering if his name was Bill or Brian or Chris or Tom. It didn't matter, it didn't matter, even though names can carry such great meaning -- like William means *the guardian* or Thomas *the twin* or George *the farmer*. To her, though, it didn't matter what his name was, only that he was real, more real than any other person she'd ever known in her long life.

She was older than him and she was going to outlive him and she could barely breathe just thinking about it. There was nothing she wanted more than to trade places with him, to put herself in the position of ending, just to save his life, just to keep him going. He was important to so many people, more than just her, and she thought it might be the most important thing she could do to keep him in the present.

But none of this is in the present. It's scattered through time, like each of their body's ashes after the cancer ate his gut, after the car left her to bleed internally.

She remembered a night, before they were lovers, before they knew what love was all about, where he'd tugged at her shirt and asked her if she wanted to fuck. She'd said no then. Instead, she'd directed him to the piano and asked him to play and he did.

"Your day breaks, your mind aches, you find that all her words of kindness linger on when she no longer needs you..." He sang and she sang along. Neither of them knew all the words to that Beatles song or any of the others they sang that night, but that didn't matter. Plus, she still needed him, despite his song choice, despite her emphatic *no*. And he still needed her.

It was the start of something.

He said he had chosen to move to the hospice care facility instead of staying in their home because he didn't want her to look at their bed and think, *he died there*. Even if he'd died on the couch. Or in the tub. Or slumped at the kitchen table. He didn't want to die there. She knew that and she respected it but she would still look at their bed and think, *he died*. He couldn't save her from that.

"You know that your garden is going straight to hell right now," she said.

"That's why this will never work out," he countered. "You're a terrible gardener."

She laughed like only she could laugh, without reservation, and pressed her hands flat on the bed next to him. "We should probably break up now."

They weren't married, hadn't ever seen the point of it, but she wished she was by his side now as a wife. She wasn't sure how that would make this all different but she knew that it would and she knew that it would be better to have that silly *Mrs.* in front of her name. Legally, she was the one responsible for his affairs once the end came, but that made it all so sterile, so unlike their life together. Like she was a guardian, someone appointed by the family or the state, not someone who *was* family, who had a moral responsibility. She had thought about asking him to marry her before he died, but she knew that wasn't the right thing to do. They weren't meant to be married. Their relationship had endured because they weren't.

For instance, if they'd been married and she'd come home to find him fucking a groupie out by the pool, she might have had to ask for a divorce and it would be messy and expensive and all over the news. But since they weren't married, she could simply tell him she needed some time and go stay in the city for awhile until they could find their way back to each other, quietly and naturally, without media and lawyers and paperwork.

She liked to think of him as Odysseus and herself as Penelope. Odysseus was seduced by many a nymph but he only loved Penelope. The whole time he traveled, he sang about his love, his undying love, for his wife, his one true soul mate, even when he fucked another woman, even when he betrayed her, he only loved her, and she knew she was Penelope and he was Odysseus, that no matter who he had on the side, he only loved her. And that was why she'd turned down his three marriage proposals, that's why she'd tell him she had to leave for awhile, that's why she always came back. She was like Penelope, weaving on the loom, avoiding other men because she knew, in her heart, that Odysseus would come home to her, always. And he did.

She had a different sensibility than him. She never strayed. never looked at another man with serious temptation. Her body belonged to him, she didn't need anyone else's fingerprints on it. She never did. No one else ever mattered. Not even before they were lovers. Not even before they knew exactly how lucky they were. And it's because she knew, could recognize, how blessed she was that she put up with the other women, the sirens, the nymphs, because they were part of his journey.

Once, before they were lovers, she'd settled in with another man and when she'd glance at her phone to see if this other man had called, he'd tap her on the arm and asked, *What are you doing? You're not leaving.* She'd smiled and assured him she wasn't going anywhere.

She wasn't going anywhere.

He reached up and touched her face, softly, along

the chin line, the way that only he could, and he said, "I love you." She pulled herself, mind and body, back into the room and she said, "I love you, too."

She had always loved him on some level. She'd taken to telling him that from the moment that she realized it, even when his current girlfriend was within earshot, even when her current boyfriend was within earshot, she'd say it, loudly, meaningfully, with her arms wrapped as tightly around him as she could. *I love you*, she'd say. *I love you.* He always loved her, too, on some level. It just took him longer to say so. Looking back, she didn't know why it took them so long to find the straight path to each other, but it did.

Looking back, she didn't know why it took her so long to do a lot of things.

"Hey," he said. "Hey there, why are you crying? I'm the one who's dying."

She hadn't realized she was crying but when she touched her cheek she could feel the wet streak. "Yeah, but I'm the one who's going to have to deal with Benny when you're gone."

"That is a reason to cry," he said.

Benny was his agent, a small, nervous, shrewd businessman who'd built him into a musical phenomenon. She already knew he was one, so did everyone who ever saw him perform, but Benny made it global. No one attacked the keys like her man and Benny made sure everyone knew.

Later when she sat down to write this story, she thought about the early days, long before Benny or the world knew about him, even before he was hers, and she loved how pure life was then. Here we are with our day jobs, part of the grind. Here we are part of the night life, part of the scene. This is how she met him, this is how she knew him, this is how she loved him. Looking back, she had the most nostalgia for those days, even though their life together was intense and wonderful, because in those days he'd been a man on a stage in a bar that was almost always half empty and just the close friends and familiar faces lined the walls and gathered near the stage. Where everybody knows your name. She grew to miss those days after he was plucked from obscurity, she along with him. As she wrote this story, she wanted to infuse that sense of purity that accompanied them at the beginning because that was really their essence, not the hoopla and glory, although those days were shimmering in her mind, too. How to fuse consciousness, she didn't exactly know.

She was learning that the recreation of these events was expansive, more expansive than anything she'd ever dared tackle before.

Before she sat down to write, she sat by his hospice bed and hummed songs by The Rolling Stones and Queen and Red Hot Chili Peppers and Beethoven. She'd told him stories from their past, as if he hadn't been there, as if she wanted to include him in his own history. He was forgetting things, she could tell, and she thought that must be part of dying: letting go of everything past and present. She wasn't ready for that yet, not for him, not for her, so she kept talking, even when he'd fall asleep and snore lightly as she laughed over mishaps at gigs, extravagant parties, intimate moments between them.

Her favorite moment was the one where she

realized that he was exactly what she wanted, a moment that came years after she knew she loved him but not yet to the full extreme. She told this story to him often and it always made him smile; she was sure he remembered it even without her telling, but she'd go on anyway.

"That night, we'd met at the bar, listened to the band, gotten drunk with our friends, and gone home together. Into your apartment and into your bed, but just to sleep. And in the morning, you got up first and then I followed suit and we sat together and talked about nothing important for the longest time. And then you looked at me and asked what I was up to that day and I saw it on your face, that change I was feeling. I told you that you were part of my plans for the day. You nodded and said let's go and off we went to errands and lunch and a strange sense of intimacy fell over me in those hours together, an intimacy that I had been missing my entire life. And when I had to go, you hugged me so tightly I could barely breathe and we said our goodbyes until later and I walked away, stunned."

Whenever she got to the end of the story, she'd feel the same old glow that she'd felt that afternoon, so many years ago, and she'd omit the balance of that story, the awkward strain of guilt she'd felt meeting up with him that night, him and his girlfriend at the time, a woman she liked, him and his girlfriend and another of their friends. Four adults around a table. He sat across from her and stared at her intently and she'd not known how to act. She never retold this part of the story because it reminded her of the darker side of their relationship. No one needed to be reminded of that while waiting for something final to happen in a hospice.

Before she'd considered writing this story, she'd made a conscious decision not to tell the entire story of their life together, not to the world. Close friends, they knew, they shook their heads and they held their breath, but they also saw the reverse, the good times, the moments of sheer ecstasy that almost validated the infidelities, the days of disappearing, the overt abuse of drugs and alcohol. Everyone has his own demons. Everyone has things to overcome.

Her greatest demon was him and everyone knew it.

Sitting beside him now, she knew that she'd made the right decision to stick with him all these years. Later when she would write this story, she wanted to make sure that was ultimately clear: this was their correct path.

"Do you remember the second time you asked me to marry you?" she asked.

He swallowed hard and said, "Mmm hmm. Mostly I remember you saying no."

"Yes, but do you remember what I said?"

"You said you loved me too much to marry me. You said that you were too happy with the way things were to accept the ring I was offering." He looked at her with a tiny smile. "You said the test came back negative."

She giggled and nodded to confirm his accurate re-telling. "I was so sure that I was pregnant that time," she said.

"You know that's not the reason I bought you a diamond," he said quietly.

She blinked.

She knew that. She knew that he'd meant it each time he'd asked and she knew she'd meant it each time she'd declined. For a fleeting moment, she always considered saying yes, she'd even considered asking him once or twice, like now in the hospice, but something always stopped her.

Her father was a fireman and had been killed on the job when she was young and her mother had never remarried. Her mother had spent the rest of her life mourning a man who was flawed but good. She had grown up watching her mother do everything alone, raise her children, clean storm drains, practice yoga. So she had grown up believing that her mother's way was both foolish and necessary and when she came of age, she saw relationships as risks too steep to take. *He'll either leave me for someone else or he'll leave me for no one else or he'll die, like my father,* she thought. Perhaps by way of a self-fulfilling prophecy, she was correct about men leaving her until she finally gave in to him. But even though she was closer to him than anyone else, she still didn't trust he wasn't going to leave.

He strayed, but he never left.

Once after a particularly bad nymph encounter, she had stayed in the city for two months and worked on a play. She loved that kind of writing, for the stage, open for interpretation, ready for direction. The play was about a man who loved a woman who wouldn't let herself love him back. At the end, the man kisses her on a dark stage under a single spotlight and he says, "If you only could." The woman looks at him and says, "If *you* only could," and she walks away, leaving him alone under that stark white light. She cried the entire time she wrote that scene and she never turned the play over to her agent. Instead, she banged out countless short stories and set to work on a short volume of poetry before settling in on a new screenplay about the life of Emily Dickinson.

He came to see her at least once a week during that two month separation, never begging her to come home but offering simple reminders of how much he loved her and making sure she had food in the refrigerator.

"I'm not a child," she'd say.

"I'm not a parent," he'd counter as he opened a bottle of wine and poured them each a glass.

Before he'd leave, each time he'd ask her if she was coming home with him that day. Each time she'd stared coolly at him and shook her head and waited until his car was well out of view before she'd slump on the floor and cry. But at the end of the two months when he asked, she said, "Yes, I think so," and they'd gotten in his car together and driven home and made love for as long as they both had the energy.

She was a Gemini and sometimes she thought this explained it all. Gemini is the Twin sign in the zodiac and they often spend their lives looking outside of themselves to find their twin. She was a textbook Gemini and often chuckled over this small fact about her sign. Until she met him. Somewhere along the way, soon after she'd met him, something calming overtook her and she knew -- he was her twin. They were quick to become close friends and the closer they grew, the more she saw him as her mirror, sometimes reflecting her exactly, sometimes reflecting her oppositely, but always reflecting.

Later, when she wrote about it all, she'd leave out the aftermath of losing an entire half of herself. She wouldn't know how completely that had happened until just before the car would strike her down in that parking lot. She wouldn't know until she thought, *I haven't been myself lately*. Blink of an eye. Done.

"You know what I like best about you. Hey," he said, tugging at her sleeve. "Looky here."

Her face softened but her gaze remained fixed out the window. "Yes, I know," she said. "Me, too."

Written in 2010

Guided Hypnosis #38

You watch her move and wonder what she was like as a child. Seeing her now, she's so free and easy, so bright with laughter. You wonder if she's ever had even so much as a skinned knee. You're charmed by her and she knows it, which is why she spins her ethereal love spell around everyone except you.

You didn't want to come tonight. You don't like this band and you don't know many of the other faces in the bar. It's dark, though, and they carry the brand of tequila you prefer, so you're sipping in silence, on a barstool tucked in the corner. You know this bartender. She's worked here about as long as the building's been standing. You sometimes joke with her that she was standing here, ready to make a cocktail and some guy came along and built the bar around her. She doesn't tell you you're wrong but she does smile in a way that makes you wonder if Santa Clause isn't real after all. Her name's Barbara and she has already made all the small talk with you that she can on this busy night. You keep her in your peripheral but you both know why you're here. Earlier, Barbara leaned over to you and nudged your shoulder. "*She* invited you, eh?" You don't even have to nod, but you do, slightly, wincing as you add, "She invited everyone."

The music starts up and it's a little better than you remember it being. You watch her swirl through the front line of gawkers, the superfans that make all of the rest of the attendees look like they're not trying hard enough. You aren't opposed to dancing or being up front to show your support, but not for this group of players. They have a

Caribbean rock sort of feel, like maybe you should be drinking Painkillers or Blue Hawaiis, some offishly named cocktail involving rum and deception.   It's only forty degrees outside, despite it being spring, because, well, New England.   You're not in the mood for this, not for any of this.

And that's when she looks right at you.   Her smile grows slowly, like one of those capsules you drop into water and it fizzles into a sponge in the shape of a dinosaur, and she starts to move towards you.   You try to maintain a neutral gaze, but you can feel your heart beat just a little more intensely in your chest.   She's getting closer and closer, her long, black hair draping around her shoulders like a gypsy shawl as her turquoise dress hangs stubbornly loose, barely moving in rhythm with her, as if on strike for what's about to transpire.   Your hand grips a little tighter around your glass of tequila as she weaves through the crowd.

Before she can get to you, though, she's stopped by someone who grabs her wrist out of nowhere and pulls her invisibly away.   You hear the unmistakable delight in her giggle as someone twirls her around and draws her in, kissing her nose with the intimacy of no lost time.   You swallow hard and down the rest of your tequila.   You signal to Barbara for the check.   "Outta here already?" she tsk's as she slides the black sleeve documenting the inventory you've consumed in the last hour.   You slide a twenty dollar bill in without checking.   You know it's enough. You don't answer Barbara's question.   Instead, you stand up a little too quickly and the bar stool clatters to the ground.

Everyone turns to stare at you. You, who had hoped to be invisible tonight, are suddenly the main event. Even the guys in the band are peering towards the commotion. You pick up the bar stool and try to turn away from the attention while Barbara says cheerfully, "Play the one about the beach!" Everyone chuckles. All of their songs are about the beach. The band starts up their next tune and you consider trying to sneak out the back door. Glancing in that direction, you can see it's crowded over there, so you resign yourself to marching out the front.

Just as you are nearly in the clear, she is suddenly right in front of you. How did she get there? You blink at her as she mimes a cigarette. She thinks you smoke because you do with her. You nod, tersely though, and she grabs your hand to lead you outside.

It's bone-chillingly cold, damp and dark, but she barely even shivers despite not having a coat. You shove your hands deep into your winter coat and feel a little ill as she pulls a pack of cigarettes out of a little pouch she carries on a long cord around her neck. She hands you one and you light it, anyway, the two of you puffing in silence for a moment or two.

"Why are you leaving?" she asks after a long exhale.

You shrug. "Why should I stay?"

She stares out at the street for a moment before looking back at you with one of those penetrating gazes that you only think you're able to decipher. You lean over and kiss her on the nose, same as you saw the stranger do before, and you stand back to see her react. She smiles briefly, puffs a little *huh*, and drops her cigarette to the ground to stub it out.

"You're cute," she says, wrapping you into a full-impact embrace.

You pull the cigarette out of your mouth, afraid it'll ash in her glossy hair, and notice the moon is a sliver in the sky. You let her hold you for as long as she wants, which feels too long, and when she finally lets you go, you sigh and start to walk away.

"Why are you leaving?" she calls after you.

You don't need to look back to know the vision of beauty she remains on the street that night, unshivering and curious about your answer, but not enough to call it out a third time.

Written in 2018

Coors Draft and a Jameson

Maddie sat heavy on the barstool with her head propped up by one hand while the other's fingers scrolled slowly through screens on her phone. "Say, where you think I can get a merkin by this weekend?"

From behind the bar, her sister June poured her a shot of Jameson and raised an eyebrow. "Dunno. Thrift shop on Bradley Street, maybe?"

Maddie unpropped her head and flicked her middle finger while she took the shot. "I'd rather go to one of those fancy crafting stores like Paper Source or Michael's and ask one of those uppity sales girls if they had the supplies to fabricate one."

"Shit, you should do that. It'd be *hilarious*," June said with a straight face.

"Think Amazon'd have a good one?" Maddie asked, back to scrolling.

"Whatcha need one for, anyway?" June asked, sliding a draft of Coors in front of her sister along with a second shot.

"Orlando's party," Maddie sighed, her entire being heavier than it was just moments before.

"Oh, that this weekend?" June asked, a slight lilt in her voice.

"Fuck you," Maddie said.

"You two play nice, now," said a voice from the shadowy doorway.

"Listen, Pap, you don't know what's what," Maddie said, taking her second shot and propping her head back up.

"So why don't you inform me," Pap said, settling his over-sized, over-smoked frame down beside her.

"Jesus, you been home in awhile?" Maddie asked, wrinkling her nose.

Pap shrugged and wiped his ever-so-slightly running nose with the back of his sleeve. "You know how Barb can be."

June slid a Coors draft and a shot in front of Pap and handed another shot to her sister before pouring one for herself. "Even I will drink to that," June said as they clinked glasses and swallowed down.

"Yeah, what's with that," Pap started, swinging his gaze towards the blonder sister. "You tapped out?"

June shrugged. "Trying on new hats, that's all," she said.

"Which reminds me..." Maddie said, tapping on her Amazon icon.

June chuckled. "You can't buy no merkin on there."

"You're in the merkin market, Maddie?" Pap asked, amused.

Maddie made a face. "I got this party this weekend..."

"You got a party where you need a merkin?" Pap guffawed. "Where's *my* invite?"

"Left it with your wife," Maddie muttered.

Pap took a swig of his Coors and shook his head at June. "You got all the sweet genes, I guess."

June leaned against the wall with her arms folded. "I guess," she echoed.

Pap turned his attention back towards the more brunette sister. "So you're looking for a crotch hat."

"Crotch wig," June corrected.

Maddie shot them both dark looks. "I got this party..."

"Since when does Orlando make you girls strip down?" Pap asked.

Maddie shrugged. "He don't always. But this weekend's... different."

"Why's that?" Pap asked.

Maddie shifted. "It's confidential."

Pap chuckled and slapped his hand on the bar. "You hear this shit, June?"

"I hear it," she said.

Maddie slowly typed *m-e-r-k-i-n* into her Amazon *search* bar. "Shiiiiit," she said through shut teeth.

"What?" June and Pap said in unison.

"They call it Kitty Carpet," Maddie said, flipping her phone around for them to see. "*This* one's called 'Michael Jackson Hair.' That shit's disgusting."

"Here's a sticker that says 'Make a Wish on My Merkin,'" June said, taking the phone from her sister. "Get one of those. It's Prime eligible."

"Fuck you," Maddie said. "Gimme another shot, why don't ya?"

"What's Prime eligible mean?" Pap asked, his eyes growing round.

"Free shipping, you perv," June said, handing her sister back her phone before pouring her another shot.

"Maybe I should get this pink one," Maddie said, holding her phone close to her face.

"Pink what?" asked El, who'd finally returned from his restock run to the basement.

"It takes you longer and longer to jack off anymore," June muttered, stalking away from the bar.

"What's her beef?" El asked.

"You were gone like fifteen minutes. Maybe she's gotta pee," Maddie said, her phone still close to her face.

"You trippin', Maddie?" El asked. "Because you seem pretty canned right now. And you wasn't at all not that long ago."

"Mind your business and pour me a shot," Maddie said.

El nodded towards Pap. "You up, too?" he asked.

Pap nodded. "Can't ask the lady to shoot alone."

"Maybe this animal print," Maddie said, carefully setting her phone back on the bar.

El slid the shot glasses in front of the patrons. "What?"

"She needs some carpet to match the drapes for a party this weekend," Pap supplied.

Maddie clinked her shot glass with Pap's and shot hers straight down. "Might be in for a promotion."

El eyed them both curiously. "How many shots y'all had?"

June returned, wiping her hands on her jeans. "What are you, inventory control?"

El clucked his tongue. "Woman, what is your beef?"

"I ain't got no beef. I'm vegan, motherfucker," June said, ripping open a turkey jerky pack from her stash behind the bar.

Pap laughed and took his shot. "She got you there."

"How you figure that?" El asked. "Damn."

"Last time," Maddie began slowly, "Orlando made us all wear tails over our cocktail waitress get ups. I wore a bunny one. Think I can turn it into a merkin? Shave it down and slap it on there with some double stick tape?"

"Problem solved," June deadpanned.

"Merkin Muffley, President of the United States?" said a new voice from the shadowy doorway.

"What?" they all said, swinging their gaze towards the arrival who sauntered in and sat down on the other side of Pap.

"Merkin Muffley is the president's name in *Dr. Strangelove*. Just watched it on cable last night."

Maddie pressed her hand against her mouth and giggled. "Really, Steve-o?"

Steve-o nodded solemnly. "You on another Merkin?"

Maddie continued to giggle. "Nothing presidential," she said.

"Merkin 9-5, what a way to make a livin'," sang El.

"Everybody's merkin for the weekend," added Pap.

"Merkin' at the carwash," crooned June.

"I've been merkin' on the railroad," sloshed Maddie.

Steve-o peeled his eyeballs around the room. "What the hell?" he asked.

"Get this man his round," Pap said, slapping a hand on Steve-o's back. "He's gotta lot of catching up to do."

El slid a Coors draft and a shot in front of Steve-o and poured another round of shots for the rest of them. "In this place, there's always someone who's gotta catch up."

"Cheers to that," they said as they clinked glasses and threw their heads back.

Written in 2013

Aliens Onboard

General Bacon was the commander of the alien spaceship and second in command was a robot named Sport. Both of them were terrified of encountering a human being, even though it was their job to seek such creatures out and study them for science. More often than not, the female on board, an alien whose name was Daffodil, would roll her extended eyes and do all the probing while General Bacon and Sport busied themselves with "paperwork," a term that made little sense in the alien world but they stuck with it anyway.

"This one wants to be taken to our leader," Daffodil would say on her more uppity days.

General Bacon would cringe and turn away, saying, "Well, I would and all, but this damned paperwork..."

Daffodil would sigh and mutter about equality in the workplace and count the days until their fact-finding mission was finally over.

"One hundred and eleven days," she'd say as General Bacon and Sport bumped their heads together while reaching for the same stack of files. "You know those are all blank, right?" she'd add.

Finally, Daffodil's count had whittled down to a mere three days and the crew was beginning to get restless since they'd not yet received new marching orders.

"You don't think we're gonna get stuck on fact-finding for another cycle, do you?" General Bacon would whisper to Sport.

"I hope not. I miss my wife," the robot muttered.

"Well, did you remember to file all the mission logs?" Daffodil inquired.

General Bacon pursed his lips. "File mission logs?" he asked.

Daffodil and Sport stared at him with their mouths hanging open. "You're joking," Daffodil said.

General Bacon scratched his head. "Well, I... Nope, I'm not kidding," he said.

"What exactly do you *do* every day?" Daffodil sputtered. "We can't be relieved of this duty until the mission logs are all filed. Have you done any?"

"Well, I... No," General Bacon admitted.

"You know the only way out of doing another cycle is to crash onto Earth, right?" Daffodil said. "They'll have to come and recover us. It's our only hope."

"But what if we see some... humans?" General Bacon said with a shudder.

"Oh, grow up," Daffodil said, snapping some latex gloves on her hands. "Let me dump the current specimen and figure out our plan."

General Bacon and Sport stared at each other.

"Why didn't you tell me I had to file mission logs?" General Bacon asked his subordinate.

"I only know what you have programmed me to know," Sport said.

"I knew I should have insisted on a robot upgrade when my contract came up for renewal," General Bacon sighed.

"Well, you get what you pay for," Sport said with a shrug.

"Yes, that's right -- you do," General Bacon said slowly. "Excuse me, I've got to go formulate a plan now."

General Bacon retreated back to his private study where he went online to check his current account balance and decided he had more than enough money to pay his own way off the mission. He set his mind to telepathically communicate with what humans offended referred to as "the mothership," and within minutes, was teleported off his craft without a word of warning.

In the meantime, Sport and Daffodil had no idea their fearless leader had totally abandoned them so they went about their daily ritual of Daffodil doing all the work while Sport idled nearby. Neither of them even seemed to notice General Bacon's absence and it was only when Daffodil realized it was the last day of the mission that she said, "Hey, Sport, seen the boss around?"

"Not for awhile," Sport said.

Daffodil scrunched her face up suspiciously and started searching the craft and when she'd looked everywhere twice, she stood dumbfounded in front of Sport. "He's gone," she said.

"Maybe he parachuted to Earth," Sport suggested. "You did suggest we should crash land on Earth and hope for rescue. Maybe he just went for it."

Daffodil's eyes narrowed down flat as the horizon. "He'd sooner eat his hat than subject himself to Earth," she said.

"That's true," Sport said. "Well, I'm out of ideas."

Daffodil shook her head. "Machines," she muttered.

"We're only as good as the martians who made us," Sport quipped.

Daffodil turned on a transmitter to bring the command center into view on the wall. No one was anywhere to be seen.

"Hello?" she asked.

Little did she know that most of those aboard the "mothership" had all come down with a wicked case of the very contagious space madness and were largely laying low and sleeping it off.

"Everyone's dead," Daffodil concluded.

"That's too bad," Sport said.

Daffodil flipped his switch to the "off" position and shoved him off to the side. "Goodbye, old hunk of metal," she said as she strapped on a parachute and flung herself out of the escape hatch to try her hand at living among the humans. She did, after all, know their ways and means quite intimately after all those years of probing. She'd make an awesome human -- she knew how to morph and fit in.

Moments after the hatch resealed behind her, General Bacon, one of the few to be well enough to be on call, wandered into view on the screen. When he recognized whose wall it was, he panicked for a moment and then ducked out of view, hitting all the correct buttons to return the ship back to home base where he discovered Sport in the off-mode and switched him back on.

Daffodil was eventually re-discovered by the aliens but by then, she'd settled into human life quite amazingly and became something of a spy. Her code name still to this day is Martha Stewart.

Written in 2013

Guided Hypnosis #29

You think this will make you happy -- this hit, this line, this shot -- so you do it and you feel nothing, so you leave your house. Outside, things are peaceful and still -- they're wrapped in the comfort of a two a.m. moon shining down on the street where so many lives are lived. None of them matter to you, though, so you stumble along, wishing for a rock or a can or a ball to kick, something to break up the silence, the monotony of you, alone with the stars you only wish the city would allow you to see. You get into your car only to sit, leaning against the wheel, your hands gripping, your face an intense swirl of aggressive indignation -- of course you have this all under control. Anyone could see that through your slack-jawed full body tremors -- anyone could see how hard you try to be a wearable mask. Day in and day out, you build the fable of your overflowing life, bursting at the seams with phrases like, "Just as I wanted," "Exactly my plan," "Conventional doesn't interest me." You get dirtier and dirtier as each stubborn word slides out of your mouth, a true defecation if there ever was one, and it leaves this cloud of stink around you that you don't even smell anymore. Around you, your *stuff*, your *life*, builds in precarious piles that teeter unceremoniously while you shrug and slide your hand up the thigh of that day's lured woman and say, "Who's got time for any of that?" You say, "Fuck *that*" and you do, but still, you are not happy. You try to tell a woman about the horrors of your dreams and she stares at you so blankly, you wonder if she's even alive. Yet, still, you cling to her, her flesh, her presence in this moment, her ability to make you not alone.   Alone now in your car, you would give anything to have even cold flesh to touch that wasn't your own.   You would give anything to feel any other way but this.   You think of someone you used to know with green eyes that made you love like you'd never loved before. You think of someone who shined like gold to you and you wonder why you buried her somewhere far away -- you wish you could dig her back up.   You press your thumb into your unclean arm and you think maybe if you wallow in this dirt you've kicked up, you'll be happy with what you've created, you'll be buried like her.   You told no one when she left you.   In fact, you smiled bigger than before. "I'm on a pursuit for happiness," you tell anyone who will listen, even if it's just you, now, in your car.   "I'll be good once I get it..."   You say this without moving, the spin out of your control.

Written in 2015

Inside the Room

The door closed.

She stirred from her fitful rest and was in a full upright sitting position before she knew what had happened. She could feel the gumminess of sleep caking her mouth, and she stifled a yawn with her hand pressed tightly against her lips. She opened her eyes after a moment and stared dully at the darkness around her. Was it Day? Was it Night? She couldn't remember much about this Place except she wasn't surprised to open her eyes to the Void.

The door closed.

She looked towards the sound and thought she heard it echoing Outside. She felt dreamlike in the darkness and the echoing made her shake her head and almost wake up to the reality of her life in a world without light. It made her lightheaded, and she went limp, her body crumpled on the floor, her arms twisted in awkward, incredibly limber contortionistic lines around her body. One arm wrapped solidly around her neck. The other jutted at an odd angle under her chin. Her torso was twisted and her legs were split and crooked. She stared into the darkness, eyes wide and glassy.

The door closed.

She rolled onto her back and pretended to make a snow angel in the blankets, a game she played often enough that she'd taken the time to imagine how ridiculous she looked: a grown woman wildly, rhythmically thrashing about in the midst of thick blankets covered in symmetrical snowflakes. If she could see the flakes in the dark, she'd make the same comment she'd make in the light: *See? Those two look alike*, thus debunking the myth that they were all -- we were all -- unique snowflakes. She stared into the darkness, her arms and legs flailing, and laughed.

The door closed.

She thought of pain and a blinding light.

The door closed.

She was Inside the Room. She wasn't sure if she'd ever been Outside, although she remembered the Trees and the Sun and the Ocean. She thought she'd heard Music once before in Nature -- Birds and Grasshoppers and all of that Nonsense. But she wasn't sure where the memory was rooted. She didn't know anything sensory except for Darkness. She was Inside the Room and it suited her fine. She got everything she needed Inside.

The door closed.

She heard someone breathing Outside. She crawled across the floor to get closer to the noise, and she began to mimic its pattern. In and Out. In and Out. In and Out. Wheeze and Cough. In and Out. Sputter and Silence.

The door closed.

She sat with her back against the wall and stretched her legs out straight in front of her. She pointed her toes like she used to in ballet classes as a child. She arched her arms over her head in a semicircle, the fingers on her opposite hands coming too close to touching to be the way her teacher had shown her. She pressed her arms against the wall and flexed her toes. It made her smile in the darkness.

The door closed.

She heard Someone knock from Outside, and it sounded violent Inside. She put her hands over her ears and ground her teeth together. *Can you hear me?* She mouthed *no*. *Do you know I'm here?* She mouthed *no*. *Let me in!* She screamed *NO!* Whoever was Outside banged and banged on the door but couldn't come in. She blinked in the darkness.

The door closed.

She yawned. She slept.

The door closed.

She was Inside, but, more than that, she was In Darkness. She *was* Darkness. It filled her pores and replaced the static in her hair and glinted off her teeth, her teeth which glowed in the Darkness. She welcomed her Fate with eager smiles and emphatic gestures. She mimed her acceptance of her Place Inside the Room with quick bows and fluttering eyelids. She wrapped the Darkness around her body like the blankets on the floor. She covered her head in Absence, and she was Happy.

The door closed.

She wasn't Alone Inside the Room. There was a scurrying of Noise along the opposite wall. She couldn't remember if she was close to the door or if the Noise was close to the door. It was too dark to tell, and she was suddenly afraid. Solitude was eroding her will to interact with Things Outside and this Intruder, this Concept of Noise, frightened her. *Go away*, she whispered. The Noise scratched the floor in time to her nail scratching the floor. *Go away*, she whispered in the dark.

The door closed.

She was Alone. There was no key to unlock her. It was dark, and she couldn't find the door, anyway. She reached her arms out in front of her to see if there was Something to Grasp in the Darkness. Inside the Room, she created her own door, her own sense of light. There was no way out unless she Thought About It.

The door closed.

She recited: *you're just too good to be true -- can't take my eyes off of you*. Someone used to sing these words to her Outside. Inside, she didn't sing the words, but she spoke them over and over. She repeated the phrase, and she didn't know why.

The door closed.

She struggled with Beginnings and Endings because how does she Begin and End? Nothing was the same Inside and all of her experiences Outside seemed extraneous to Now. The Room Inside owned her. She held out her wrists to No One and waited. She cried in the darkness. She

laughed.
　　The door closed.

Written in circa 2000

Say You'll Love Me

The scene is a modern kitchen with sparse furniture -- just a white table with three chairs. Music plays, banal, like something heard in a supermarket. It is appallingly early, as is evidenced by a rumble of snoring heard off stage. There is a light hanging over the table that is turned on and casting a soft glow over the space. The stage remains empty for a solid five minutes with nothing else happening. Until...

From off stage right, ALEX slides a thick, heavy book across the floor and the music and snoring stop. Everything remains silent and still for another full minute before CHRISTINE, dressed all in black, enters from stage left. She walks tiredly across the kitchen and slumps in one of the chairs, propping her head up on her hand.

CHRISTINE *(singing)*

Unbreak my heart, say you'll love me again. Undo this pain that you caused when you walked out the door and walked out of my life. Uncry these tears...

She pauses when she notices the book on the floor. She stares at it but she doesn't move. She also doesn't resume singing. Another long silence lingers until ALEX enters from stage right. He's wearing pajamas and a baseball hat.

ALEX

Toni Braxton kind of night?

CHRISTINE doesn't look at him but continues to stare at the book.

CHRISTINE

I heard a man on a bicycle singing it outside just now. It's stuck in my head.

ALEX leans against the stage right entrance and stares at her.

ALEX

A man on a bicycle?

CHRISTINE

Yes, a man on a bicycle. He was riding past me on my way home from work and he was singing that song. *(A pause)* I think he was crying. *(Another pause)* I wish you'd been there -- you'd have loved it.

CENTER: ALEX

The song or the crying?

CENTER: CHRISTINE

All of it.

ALEX shoves off his leaning post and goes over to sit across the table from her.

CENTER: ALEX

How was the bar tonight?

CENTER: CHRISTINE

Same as always.

CENTER: ALEX

How did the mortifying project go?

CHRISTINE looks over at him for the first time.

CHRISTINE

Mortifyingly.

ALEX

Say more...

CHRISTINE

It's late. I should go to bed.

ALEX

It's early. Stay awhile.

CHRISTINE *(sighs)*

There's not much to say about the project.   The photographer seemed professional and we got it done and that's all that really should matter at four in the morning.

ALEX

Did you get the bonus?

CHRISTINE *(nodding)*

In cash.

ALEX

Well, that'll buy you some pleasurable life moments if you spend it wisely.

CHRISTINE

When have I ever done that?

ALEX *(laughing)*

It's a new day.

CHRISTINE

Not according to what my body is telling me. I really should go to bed.

CHRISTINE gets up and starts to walk past ALEX, who stands up so fast he knocks his own chair over in the process. He isn't touching her but she jerks back as if he's grabbed her arm.

ALEX

How's Doug?

CHRISTINE

Fine.

ALEX and CHRISTINE stare at each other for an uncomfortably long time before both of them relax a degree and CHRISTINE keeps walking off stage right.

ALEX sees the book on the floor and sits down beside it. He holds it up so the audience can see it's The Complete Works of William Shakespeare.

ALEX *(reading)*

Call up Lord Stanley, bid him bring his power. I will lead forth my soldiers to the plain, and thus my battle shall be ordered. (A pause) Go, gentleman, every man unto his charge. Let not our babbling dreams affright our souls. Conscience is but a word that cowards use, devised at first to keep the strong in awe.

CHRISTINE returns from stage right, dressed in sweatpants and a long sleeve t-shirt, and leans where ALEX leaned before.

CHRISTINE

Doug's not going through with the divorce.

ALEX doesn't divert his eyes from the book, though he does set it down, still open.

ALEX

Is that what he told you after he handed you your cash bonus?

CHRISTINE moves across the stage, picks up the chair ALEX upturned, and sits there, nearly squarely behind him.

CHRISTINE

Yes.

ALEX

So what about the divorce you asked from me? Is that off now, too?

CHRISTINE

Don't be so dramatic. We're not even married.

ALEX *(gently closing the book)*

Yes, dear. I'll rephrase: is this you asking to take me back?

CHRISTINE

I don't know.

ALEX

Frailty, thy name is woman.

CHRISTINE

You would quote Hamlet at a time like this.

ALEX

At a time like what?

CHRISTINE

At a time before time should be. Why are you awake? Were you waiting for me?

ALEX

You know I have been waiting for you for a very long time.

CHRISTINE gets up from the chair and comes to sit cross-legged next to ALEX. They do not look at each other but both stare straight out at the audience.

CHRISTINE

I'm sorry. *(A pause)* About what happened.

ALEX

I know.

CHRISTINE *(turning her head to look at him)*

I don't know what to say.

ALEX *(turning his head to look at her)*

Say you'll love me.

CHRISTINE (kisses him earnestly and then whispers)

I can't.

With their eyes still fixed on each other, the music from the start of the scene begins again as they sit, seemingly frozen in time as the lights dim slowly and fade to black.

END OF SCENE

Written in 2013

Guided Hypnosis #26

"He will say something like, well, you lose some, you lose
some.
You are supposed to laugh. Exhale. Blow your nose. Flick
off the lights.
Have a sense of humor, he will whisper into the black.
Have a heart."
~ Lorrie Moore, "How"

You are lost in your thoughts. Nothing but the hum of electronics powered down in the room with you. Where do you go? Deeper and deeper into the closets of memories, days and times you haven't tried on in years -- isn't it time to make a donation to GoodWill and be done with it? You are lying down on the floor, staring at the ceiling. Your bed is right there -- all you need to do is climb in, tuck under, let go. All you need to do is get up and walk out, feel the late night rain on your skin. All you need to do is pinch that spot behind your ear that stings you to life. But all you actually do is lay there and think...and think...and think. You feel your heart beat steadily in your chest. You put your hand over it. You will suddenly hear that voice in your head once more, that laugh. You will hold your breath in an attempt to drown it out. *Was I happy then?* you will wonder and you will still not know the answer to this question you've asked a hundred times. It's been so many years, anyway, so what's the difference? Happy or not, you've continued to *be,* your cells continuing to grow, your body a factory of blood and saliva and fat and muscle and bone -- you are used to standing in front of the mirror and practicing your smile for when you must see the world. But is it really practice? And is it really a smile? Is what you're practicing to be human? You think so. You tell yourself as much. You leave your hand on your heart while your other hand explores your face, feeling all the contours and imperfections and you feel suddenly in awe of all that makes you an animal that has evolved in just this way. Does a house cat care about how others see it? Does a raccoon reflect on his choices? Does a mosquito wonder why it's here?

You close your eyes.

What's the best use of a moment, anyway? What's the best use of a life? What's the best use of a love? What's the best use of memories? No one seems to know, least of all you. That thought makes you laugh, just a little, a rumble of noise to break up the electronic quiet. You sit straight up and open your eyes.

You lose some, you lose some.

It's become a motto for you since that night, the last you spent with that particular love, here in this very room, curled in this very bed. It had been doomed from the start, anyway. But for you, all love is. What made this one different was the certainty of that phrase -- *You lose some, you lose some.* There's nothing to win, anyway. Not before that night and not after. Your cells continue to cycle through, your brain continues to think and think. Your body gets you up in the morning and pushes you through your day and reminds you to sleep every night. You feel what you feel but what's the difference? You still have to pay your rent and drink plenty of water. You still have to participate. Your broken heart will still pump blood.

You get up and slide under the covers. You close your eyes once more. You ask your brain to quiet down. What it does, though, is start to play a quiet song you used to dance to. You smile. You warm. You know there's plenty to be gained. Especially now when it's time to go to sleep.

Written in 2017

Body and Soul

I died a few years ago. It happened suddenly, like I'd always hoped it would, and, just like that, my soul snapped free from my earthly tether and along with it, my heart. What was left of my body was a shell, hollowed and then consumed by the breakdown of cells into dust. You showed me a video once of this happening to a baby pig, its carcass left on a wooden floor as a time-lapsed camera showed the stages of its post-life metamorphosis. How quickly it's over once nature has decided it's over. That's what happened to me when I died.

Before I died, I brought light with me everywhere I went. I took raw sugar cookie dough and stamped it into shapes of seasonal creatures to decorate with frosting. Sometimes, you helped. Others did, too. This was a way we passed the time while someone else made family-style dinners of lasagna and bread straight from the oven and bowls of brightly colored salads made with the best produce we could find and fresh mozzarella on top of everything as bottomless glasses of wine were poured. This was a happy existence full of music and love and family we'd chosen for ourselves. I don't mean to summarize my entire existence prior to my death to be a continuous meal, but in many ways it was. Love feeds us just as much as food, I think, so maybe it's a metaphor that applies to the big picture.

The thing about sugar cookies, though, is they're hard work. It's hard to make those shapes without ripping off a leg or a head and it's hard to bake them so they're not burnt. The reason it became my job to do this is I have the patience of a thousand of you and it was your idea to put me in this role. "Because someone's gotta do it, right?" you'd always say with a wink and a hug. And I loved you and I wanted to be agreeable, so I did it and though it was a struggle at first, I became an expert at it in no time flat. I would splatter flour on the counter and beam at anyone who came to admire or help out. Our kitchen was a bright spot, always. The lighting was only a small part of the reason why.

The last sugar cookies I made were fall-themed -- pumpkins and scarecrows and husks of corn. I made them alone in the kitchen one day when no one was around. Things had already started falling apart inside of me, though I barely understood it then. I heard your voice in my head in that new tone you'd adopted telling me how wrong I was about things that didn't need to matter but grew increasingly more crucial until you took over completely and I nearly disappeared. "This is how you feel," you'd tell me. "And you're wrong for feeling that way." I'd blink at you and open my mouth to protest or defend myself or do really anything but I didn't know how to tell you how it felt to be hit by that bus you drove into me day after day as you told me it was my foot on the gas pedal and it was all my fault. Another metaphor, yes -- I learned early and repeatedly that man can live by metaphor alone. As I rolled out the cookie dough, I thought about how wrong I must be to feel this way. Every pinch was my soul tearing free. It hurt so bad it sometimes forced me to stagger my weight against an immovable thing. Once it forced me to stagger my weight against you but you'd looked at me with a new, cold depth in your eyes and moved away to watch me fall to the ground, so I only anchored on what was going to steady me not out of loyalty but out of inanimate purpose. This counter where I rolled out my dough was becoming my new best friend, especially now that you weren't interested in playing the part. And on that day I made pumpkins and scarecrows and corn all alone, the light I brought with me everywhere was almost completely burned out and the cookies crumbled when I tried to frost them and nothing was right anymore.

When you came home that day, you barely even looked at me let alone touch me as you surveyed the mess I'd left behind in the kitchen, muttering to yourself. Without saying anything I could understand, your tone alone pinched and tore at my soul as I curled in a ball in the next room where it was dark and cold and soon after you stopped speaking and left me alone, that's when it happened. That's when I died.

That's when I had the first of what turned into a series of nightmares involving trust issues. In this one, I drove us to a party and you sat in the passenger's seat with your body pressed as far away from mine as humanly possible and you told me everything I was doing wrong. "You should've turned there. You should've made that light. You should've worn a different dress. You should've brought a nicer bottle of wine." By the time we got to the party, we went in through opposite doors and though we weren't in the same room, I could hear your voice nearby, though never clearly, and I forced a smile on my face as my soul pinched and pinched and it wasn't until the end of the dream when we stood side-by-side silently washing dishes that I finally spoke to you. I said, "Are we ever going to talk about what's happening between us?" And you'd smirked at me in a way I'd come to expect in recent days and you said, "No," and you left me there alone. When I woke up, I was heavy and dark. Oh, my soul, how it pinched even though it had already left my body.

I read a Colombian love story once where the main character said that a missing love is like having an amputated arm -- sometimes you think you can still feel it even when it's gone. After I died, I wondered if that's how you felt at all. It's how I felt. But I still moved through every day and tried to find ways to replicate that light I once brought with me everywhere and people still nodded and smiled politely at my ghost and offered me a seat at the table though I was never the same and neither were they.

You, you didn't see me at all. You just learned to walk right through me as if I were a movable wall.

Written in 2013

The Whistling Stranger

The old man spent his morning sitting on a rocker on his front porch. This was typical, as noted by the automatic head turning of paperboys and dog walkers and people on bicycles. "Good morning, Mr. Luis," they'd call, one after another. He'd lived in that town for a very long time. He'd lived in that house since he'd moved to that town when he was a young man of nineteen. No one knew where he'd come from -- one day, he'd showed up on the morning train and whistled his way to the house. He had the documents saying it belonged to him. The rumor was he was the love child of a wealthy oil tycoon in California who'd bought the house and cast his son out to live there. But anyone who asked Mr. Luis would get the "My grandfather built this house after the war against the Mexicans and when he died, he left it to me" response. It didn't matter which story was true. Mr. Luis was a kind, soft spoken man that the community loved.

And everyone loved seeing him out on his porch in the morning. The days he didn't make it out would often cause neighbors to come by with casseroles and soup and bottles of medicine they thought would be helpful for any of a variety of elderly ailments. He would welcome the guests into his home and accept their offers to help but there wasn't anything wrong with him. Some days he just preferred to stay out of the heat.

This day was more typical because out he was, on his rocker, smoking an antiquated pipe. Typical, that is, until a stranger got off the morning train and set off down the road towards the old man. An unexpected, uninvited guest who whistled his way past the townspeople and right up to the front walk of Mr. Luis' house.

The stranger was young, maybe nineteen, twenty, with a flashy scar across his right cheek. Mr. Luis had a similar scar on his left cheek, remnants of a bar fight he never quite recalled. The stranger had a single bag slung from his back and he wore a dirty white t-shirt with dusty jeans and his shaggy black hair that fell over his eyes. And he stood, feet firmly planted, at the head of the walkway as he whistled "Fools Rush In."

The pipe fell out of Mr. Luis' mouth as the stranger continued to whistle. His neighbor Mrs. Carter walked by with her labrador retriever Gem and eyed the stranger. "Mornin' Mr. Luis," Mrs. Carter called. "Mornin' stranger," she said to the boy.

"Mornin' Mrs. Carter," Mr. Luis said slowly. The stranger said nothing.

Mrs. Carter hesitated for a moment but Gem pulled her onward.

Mr. Luis swallowed hard and squinted his eyes. "Can I help you, son?"

The stranger remained stock still, except for his pursed lips whistling "Don't Be Cruel."

Mr. Luis shifted in his chair and leaned out to see if he could get a better look at the boy. "Do I know you, son?"

At this, the stranger stopped whistling and smiled. "Yessir." His voice was thick, almost heavy.

Mr. Luis swallowed hard again. "Well, state your business," he said.

The stranger remained stock still and silent for a

moment. "Don't you know?" he asked.

Mr. Luis sat back in his chair and rocked it a bit. "Can't say that I do, son. I know everyone around here."

The stranger seemed to be chuckling quietly to himself before a fresh stillness came over him. "Yes," he said.

Mr. Luis had had about enough. He stood up and held onto the porch railing to steady himself. "Yes?" he repeated. "Son, I think it's best you tell me who you are and why you're here."

The stranger nodded once. "Yes," he said again.

Mr. Luis tried to let go of the railing and move off the porch but suddenly felt dizzy so he sat back down. "You'd best come closer," he said warily. "I don't have all day to play this game."

He did have all day to play this game and the stranger seemed to know it because he remained where he was for a good solid minute before advancing up the path to the old man's house. The stranger stopped at the bottom of the stairs and looked up at Mr. Luis.

Mr. Luis could barely believe it.

The stranger was like looking at himself, back through time. Just as he'd been when he was that age.

"What's your name, son?" Mr. Luis asked.

"Most people call me Lou," the stranger said. "But I don't know why. My given name's Solomon Gray."

Mr. Luis couldn't stop staring. "Is that so."

The stranger nodded. Once. "Met a man in Dallas with a handlebar mustache who said I should come here to this town. Gave me your address. Said you'd be here. Mr. Luis, right? He said you'd be on this porch and I wasn't to come close until you asked."

The old man rested back in his rocker. "And so you just did it?"

The stranger nodded. Once.

"Why'd you do that?" Mr. Luis asked.

The stranger stared at the old man through his stone black messy hair. "The man who told me about you, he was a prophet."

At this, Mr. Luis blurted a loud round of laughter. "A prophet? Son, are you here to sell me a clock tower or add my name to a manifesto?"

The stranger was unmoved. "No. He sent me here to tell you something."

"Well, I suppose you'd better get on with it," Mr. Luis said, now at ease.

"The prophet said your day was fast approaching," the stranger said, each word like a well-placed foot step.

Mr. Luis eyed him curiously. "My day?"

The stranger nodded. "Yes."

"Did he elaborate on that?"

The stranger shook his head. Once.

Mr. Luis put the pipe back in his mouth. "Well, ok," he said. "Thanks for the news. Can I offer you a cup of black coffee?"

The stranger shook his head. "No, sir. I'll be on my way now." And off he went, whistling "Heartbreak Hotel." The old man watched him trundle off down the road towards the town's only inn as an uncanny sense fell over him.

Two days later, Mr. Luis settled into his rocking chair to read the paper and watch the town drift by and he came across an article of interest on the bottom of the front page: SOLOMON "LOU" GRAY CAUGHT SHOPLIFTING. Ahh, the stranger. The article went into the briefest of details about how this Lou character pocketed a loaf of bread and some slices of cheese and was now being held in the town jail. When the old man's neighbor Mrs. Carter walked by with Gem, he called out, "Say, Mrs. Carter, did you hear about this?"

Mrs. Carter had tied Gem to Mr. Luis' front porch and sat down for a spell to say what she'd heard. Apparently, the stranger had enough money in his wallet to pay for the items he was stealing and hadn't made much of an effort to conceal his crime. "A real vagabond," Mrs. Carter clucked.

"That was the same boy who showed up here the other day," Mr. Luis said.

His neighbor leaned back. "Yes, I thought so... Well, I'd best be on my way with Gem," she said.

Mr. Luis watched her go and decided to go to the jail himself to see what the stranger was doing. It had been a long time since he'd ventured much further then the corner store (the same one that fell victim to the stranger's robbery). Mr. Luis put on his best suit and walked slowly with a cane the eleven blocks to the jail, refusing the offers for rides from neighbors passing in cars.

The police sergeant on duty let the old man back to the holding cell without question and left the old man and the boy alone.

"You came," the stranger said.

The old man nodded. "You don't seem that surprised."

"The prophet told me you'd come," the stranger said.

The old man shifted and cleared his throat. "Well, here I am."

The stranger stood up and walked close to where the old man stood outside the cell. He held out his hands, palms flexed. "Hold out your hands," he commanded.

The old man shifted nervously again and said, "Well, I... Why?"

The stranger remained confident and still. "Hold out your hands."

The old man reluctantly obliged. "Well," he said.

The stranger pressed his palms into the old man's. "Close your eyes," he said.

The old man did and was immediately jolted into the past. He was at a deli in Dallas and a strange man with a handlebar mustache and a shiny pocket watch sat down next to him at the counter and told him in a soothing voice to get on a train to a small town called Cora and go to the house at this address and wait for the old man who lived there to invite him in. After that, the man told him to go to the local inn for a day and then attempt to rob the corner store and the old man would come from the house at the address he'd specified and allow him to press their hands together and when their eyes would open, only one of them would be left -- just the young man -- who would be freed from the jail and returned to the house where he would live until a ripe old age. Without opening his eyes, Mr. Luis staggered against the bars of the jail cell and he remembered this all happening before, to him, as a young man, being imprisoned and waking up at the house where he would live the rest of his life.

The stranger opened his eyes and was inside the old man's house. It was a fresh, sunny morning. He immediately went outside to the front porch and sat down. Paperboys and dog walkers and people on bicycles automatically turned their heads towards him and called out, "Mornin' Lou." He rocked slowly in the chair and brushed the black hair out of his eyes and started to whistle.

Written in circa 2000

Guided Hypnosis #31

"So that's how you found me
rain falling around me
looking down at a worm
with a long way to go --"
~ Ani DiFranco

You're pulled to your feet by a faceless smile, gently unpressing you from the sidewalk where you'd resigned to dwell engulfed by rain. He is a man, you think, and your unfocused eyes take him in at his worth. *Hello* you say in the language you think he speaks. He says *Hello* back all the same, but with a much more convincing accent. You trail after him as he leads, beckoning you to follow him to the shop on the corner where there's an awning to shield you both. He's got a hat at least -- your hair is plastered to the sides of your face, fat bobbles of water dripping methodically off the end of your nose. You don't know when you'll come down from this high -- this high of being *here. now.* You took something for the pain hours ago, maybe days, and it was only the snaking water that seemed to understand you until this moment with this man whose features were drawing softly into focus the harder you concentrated. He says more words to you but you don't understand them, so you press your finger to that sacred spot between his eyes and you say *Hello* once more. He blinks at you in slow motion as you gesture for a pen, something to write with, and he withdraws a blue sharpie from an inside pocket. You flip his hand over and start to draw a map of where you've come from and where you're going. It's squiggly and follows the natural creases of his palm. You turn his hand around to him and point at your work. *Hello* you say once more. All you can see are his eyes, blue and grey and green. All he does is smile with them. You stand there in the soft glow of the street light listening to the soulless music of the modern day pulse out of the convenience store. If you went in there, you'd be assaulted by fluorescent lights and the harangue of this language you'll never understand, but you won't enter. You don't have to. He stands so still in front of you, his eyes searching you so deeply that you tingle. He wants something profound from you. He wants it so much, you wonder if you've already given it to him. You tilt your face and brush your lips gently against his. You're wet from the rain. You take a step back and say the only other thing you can: *Thank you very much*. He yanks at you now, a little hard, and examines you thoroughly. You let him. Your mind escapes back to the night crawler he'd pulled you away from a few minutes ago. So many the miles of unobservable distance. So great the challenge of quantifying love. You're possessed by this grief, this shock of circumstance, this lost chance to observe nature without challenge. He lets you go as you think this and you feel yourself spin in the resolve of what this night has brought you, drowned by the circumstance of being alive.

Written in 2017

Love, Crazy Love (and Employment)

"Mary, I think I'm going to quit my job."
He said it casually, half-yawning, as he turned the

page in the Sunday morning business section. Mary's eyes lifted from their deep focus on the crosswords puzzle in front of her, and she stared at her husband. His bald head glowed dully in the yellowish light of the kitchen. He was intently reading an article about a new Macy's Vice-president. She narrowed her eyes and cleared her throat just enough to make noise.

"Pardon, love? Did you say you were going to quit your job?"

He pressed his hands flat on the table and tapped his thick fingers on the stained oak breakfast table she'd purchased at Pottery Barn eight months ago. "Yes, dear."

Mary sat up a little straighter. "You intend to leave your place of employment?"

"Yes, dear."

"Is this because of the promotion?" Her thin voice raised slightly, like steam not quite sure if the tea kettle was ready to whistle.

"I didn't get the promotion."

"Yes, dear, I know."

Harold grunted and said nothing.

Mary cleared her throat. "Because if this is because of the promotion, don't you think you should speak to..."

"No."

"No?" Mary's tiny chest heaved. "For your own sake, darling, I think you should speak to..."

"No."

"But you've worked for them for so long..."

"Piss on Holstein and Lowry," Harold said.

"Darling, really. You've been a top executive there for years, it seems to me, and maybe you just need to speak to..."

"No."

"Harold." Her thin voice deadened, and she attempted to balance the smile properly on her lips. "For your own sanity, darling, that's all I'm saying. You've invested so much of your life --"

"Thirty goddamn years. You can't buy loyalty like that these days." Harold's nostrils flared, and he stared at an article about an impending workers' strike at an industrial plant upstate.

"No, love, of course you can't. But Holstein and Lowry is your *life*. You can't quit your *life*, can you?"

"I think I'm going to."

Her lips pursed. "That's ridiculous," she said.

"Oh." Harold sighed.

Mary's eyes widened. "What do you mean *oh*? Do you think it's wise to leave your job? You're not exactly a young man."

Harold turned the page in the newspaper.

"You're not exactly *twenty*, love, that's all I mean. And if you're not twenty and willing to work for nothing, no one will want you."

"Who says I want someone to *want* me?"

"For your own sake, of course you want someone to *want* you. It's only natural."

"Then I must be unnatural because I don't give a rat's ass if some other company *wants* me."

"Well, now you're just being silly. We...we have a *way of life*, Harold. Have you forgotten? If you quit your job, we'll be penniless."

"Don't be so dramatic." He yawned again.

Mary stood up quickly and folded her thin arms tightly against her tiny chest. "I'm *not* being dramatic," she said. "I'm being realistic. If you quit your job, how will we pay our bills? We have *obligations*."

"We won't be penniless," Harold said.

"We will, though, don't you see? Odessa Fitswallace was telling me just the other day that she saw a homeless person outside the Waldorf Astoria that *could have been* the very image of Gloria Stouffer. Her husband quit his job, and then he *died* and left her with *nothing*." Mary paused to gulp in a panicked breath of air.

"Gloria Stouffer? Isn't that the one with the lisp?" Harold asked.

"Yes, dear. We mustn't focus on her handicap, though. She's now the *image of homeless* and begging for quarters outside of the Waldorf Astoria," Mary said, her noise tilting in the air.

Harold laughed. "I forgot myself."

Mary continued. "If you leave your job, we won't be able to pay our mortgage and we'll have to move in with Martin and Cathy and those children --"

"Our grandchildren?" Harold briefly glanced at her before ducking his head back towards the page.

Mary huffed. "Yes, our *grand*children. Aren't they grand? They're awful children."

"It was just a tablecloth, love," Harold said.

"It was not *just* a tablecloth, dear. It was my mother's *hand-made* lace table cloth that her mother gave to her. It's from *England*, for crying out loud. And those children *ruined* it."

"They were just being children."

Mary began tapping her toe. "They cut it with kitchen scissors! Martin and Cathy have no control..."

"They do the best they can."

"Well, if *that* is the *best*..."

"They're not bad parents."

"It was an *heirloom*, Harold!"

"It was a piece of cloth, Mary."

Mary stopped tapping her toe. "I don't want to be forced to move in with those horrible children."

"Our grandchildren."

"Yes, our grandchildren."

"Well, OK. We won't, then."

"But when we're penniless, we'll have to, don't you see? I won't beg for quarters outside of the..."

"I promise we won't. We'll live in the Mission

Street Church basement first." Harold traced his finger along the lines of an article about the rising level of young executives.

Mary's mouth formed a tight *O*. "We...will...not!"

"No?"

"That place is *filthy* and for *homeless* people who *don't bathe* and *didn't go to college*. Evelyn Brewster volunteers there every other Thanksgiving, and she said it's just awful. Really, Harold, the *Mission Street Church*?"

"Would you rather move in with Martin and Cathy?"

Mary stared at the soft glare off the freckled skin on his head. "Martin would never allow his mother to live in a homeless shelter."

"So you're saying you'd prefer to live with him?"

Mary stomped her frail foot, but the action's dramatic effect was lost because of the puffy pink slippers, recently purchased at Lord and Taylor, on her feet. "I'd prefer to live in my own home. Here, Harold."

"Yes, but when we're penniless and homeless after I quit my job, and our only options, since you've refused the Waldorf Astoria, are the Mission Street Church or our son, his wife, and their three horrible children, what do you choose?" Harold looked up at her.

"What a horrible thing to say," Mary said, pressing her hands against the table, her toothpick arms trembling under the pressure of the weight of her lithe body. "What a *horrible* thing to say. You might as well suggest I go live in Central Park."

"*We* go live in Central Park." Harold licked his fingers and turned the page.

"We?"

"Yes, *we'd* go live in Central Park. Penniless and homeless and too good to live with our son, his wife, and our three beastly grandchildren and far too elite to live in the Mission Street Church basement -- or the Waldorf

Astoria, for that matter."

"Oh, Harold... You are impossible!"

"Seems to be the case."

Mary folded her arms back across her chest and recommenced tapping her toe. "How can you sit there so calmly? Have you even thought about any of the consequences?"

"Of what?"

Mary rolled her eyes and let out an exasperated sigh. "Of *quitting* your job."

"Oh, that."

"Yes, that!"

"Consequences?" Harold looked up at the ceiling and scratched his bald head.

"Consequences!"

"I guess I haven't."

Mary sat back down and tried to smile. "Well, do please start."

"Love, I just wouldn't know how."

"Well, *I* know how! First, we'll be penniless --"

"And living in Central Park," Harold said.

"*Do* be serious," Mary said. She picked up the pencil she used for her daily crossword puzzle and tapped it on the table.

"Certainly," Harold said.

"We'll be penniless. And we have certain obligations..."

"Yes," Harold said.

"Not just to the bill collectors, either, love." Her eyes flew around the room until they settled triumphantly in the corner. "Have you forgotten about Sebastian?"

Harold's face immediately flattened, and he stared back at the newspaper. "Damn dog."

"Sebastian needs his hair done every month, Harold, or no one will know he's a poodle." Mary looked lovingly at the small, gray dog, curled and shivering, lying on a plush, red velvet pillow with *Mama's Baby* embroidered in gold.

"Well," Harold said. "If we're living in poverty in Central Park, maybe we shouldn't keep Sebastian. We could just give him to Martin."

Mary sharply drew in a breath and placed a dismayed hand against her chest. "Oh, *no*, love. Those horrible children..."

"They didn't mean to put gum in his hair, Mary."

"Or feed him bits of chocolate when they *know* it's not good for him?"

"They also didn't mean to shut him in the closet."

"Or drop his toys in the toilet bowl?" Mary leaned down and clicked her fingers at the old dog whose ears pricked up at the familiar call.

Harold laughed as the arthritic dog moved stiffly towards Mary. "I forgot they did that," he said.

Mary picked Sebastian up and gently stroked his head. "Well, I didn't."

Harold continued to laugh. "Those kids are pretty funny, love."

"They're awful. And I won't have Sebastian living with them."

Harold stopped laughing and grunted. "He can't exactly live in the park with us, you know."

Mary's eyes flared. "Sebastian's why you can't quit your job, dear. Can't you see? He'd be homeless, and he's too old to start over with a new family."

"Sort of like us, eh, toots?" Harold winked.

Mary clucked her tongue. "Focus on Sebastian, love."

"Of course, dear."

"He needs us not to be penniless. He needs his monthly haircut, and he needs us to protect him from those monster children..."

"Our grandchildren," Harold corrected.

"Our grandchildren, yes," Mary said. "You need to stay at your job for him."

"But he's a dog, and I'm a man."

"And?" Mary raised her eyebrows.

"And that means that he's supposed to bring me my slippers -- he's supposed to work for me, not the other way around."

"But, Harold..."

"No, Mary, I can't stay in this job for him."

Mary sputtered. "Well, what about our weekly dinner at the Rainbow Room? Won't you miss the entrees at the Rainbow Room?"

Harold's eyes returned to the newspaper. "Not particularly."

Mary's hand paused in mid-air above Sebastian's head. "*Excuse* me?"

"I said, 'not particularly.'" Harold yawned.

"We've been going there ever since you got your job, love, this job that has carried us from fast food to five star, world class dining. How can you say you won't miss the entrees at the Rainbow Room?"

Harold flicked at an invisible fly near his ear. "It's just food."

"...*Just* food?"

"Yes."

"But, Harold..."

"Mary, I'm not staying in a job that makes me miserable for the sake of the dog or for a five-star meal. There are more important things in life."

"Like what?"

Harold looked at her. "I don't know, love."

Mary squinted. "My mother warned me about this."

"About what?"

"That you'd do this one day."

"Do what?"

"Go crazy. She said, 'Don't marry that fool-man,

Mary Louise Simpson. Don't do it. For all his University of Virginia MBAs and charming smiles and glittery promises of a stable future, he'll just end up crazy like his mother.'"

Harold grinned. "Dear old Mom."

"'Crazy,' love. My mother warned me that you'd go crazy, but she never could have known it would be at Sebastian's expense." She held the dog up so his old, wobbly legs hung limply in the air.

"She should have had the foresight."

"You know she had a bad heart." Mary set Sebastian back on her lap.

"So that affected her visionary powers?" Harold asked.

Mary hesitated. "My mother said you'd go crazy, just like your mother, and leave me penniless..."

"And begging for quarters outside of the Waldorf Astoria?" Harold offered.

"*Yes.* She told me not to marry you. She said it would only lead me to ruin."

"She always was an intuitive old broad."

"*Harold.* Speak respectfully of my mother."

"It's the inherited crazy germ speaking, not me," Harold said. His eyes rested on an article about an up-start internet company.

"Oh, do you think Martin will catch it, too?" Mary asked suddenly.

"Definitely." Harold yawned.

"Well, no wonder he's an unfit parent."

Harold chuckled. "Martin is not an unfit parent."

"Oh, what do you know? You're crazy."

Harold nodded. "Seems to be the case."

Mary set Sebastian on the floor and stood up. "Maybe I should call the doctor..."

Harold's head shot up. "I don't need a doctor."

"Not for *you.* For Martin. There's still a chance for him." Mary picked up her address book from its nook on the counter and began thumbing through the pages. "Dina Lowell's daughter went quite batty when she went to college, and Dina found just the most precious doctor. Fixed her right up."

"The daughter?"

Mary's fingers stuck on a page, and she waved her free hand at Harold. "Oh, no. Dina. She felt *so awful* that her daughter had to be locked up -- guilty, like it was her genes or bad mothering or something -- but it turned out the daughter was just addicted to drugs."

"Well, thank god for that," Harold said.

Mary paused. "You don't think *Martin* does drugs do you?"

"No," Harold said.

"Well, maybe that's why he's such an unfit parent."

"He doesn't do drugs."

Mary studied Harold. "No, he definitely inherited his crazy parenting ideas from you."

"Thank you."

"Oh, I can't find that number. I'll have to call Dina later. Martin's been crazy since birth, I'm sure of it. He can wait a few more hours." Mary sat back down and stared intently at Harold. She reached across the table and took his massive hands into her own. He paused in his reading, clearly startled that she'd interrupted his fingers from tracing along the words on the page, and stared at her. She smiled sweetly. "Love, is this why you want to quit your job? Is it the insanity?"

Harold deadpanned. "Yes."

Mary nodded sympathetically. "I was afraid of that."

"I figured."

"Love, I'll take care of you. I'll make sure you don't miss any buttons when you dress in the morning, and I'll pack you your favorite lunch every day, and I'll make sure no one finds out that you've lost your mind." Her voice was laced with strychnine and saccharine. "No one has to know. I'll protect you."

Harold raised his thick eyebrows. "Oh, really?"

Mary nodded her tiny head. "Of course, love. You may not be the man I married thirty-two blissful years ago, but you're what's left of him, and we made vows. Those were serious."

Harold smiled. "Weren't they though?"

"Oh, yes. And I'm very nurturing. Everyone says so. I can help you."

"That's good to know."

"I can start now."

Harold eyed her warily. "OK."

She squeezed his hands and then let them go. "I'll make you some honey tea."

"Because that will soothe my insanity?"

"It can't hurt!" Mary sang.

"Listen, Mary, before you get too carried away here... About my job," Harold began.

Mary turned away from the stove where she'd just placed the tea kettle on the burner. "Yes, that's been settled, hasn't it?"

"Has it?"

"We agreed that you'd stay in your job, and I'd protect you from having your coworkers discover your mental deterioration. Trust me, love."

"We agreed?"

"Yes, love."

"Seriously? You think a crazy man should be an executive?" Harold leaned back in his chair.

"No, I think crazy men should be pro-bono lawyers," Mary said seriously. "But, as I've said, we have a way of life... And Sebastian..."

"Enough with the dog!"

"All right, darling. Stay calm. The tea will be ready shortly."

Harold stared at her, his jaw slightly gaped, his eyes wide and round. He began to shake his head slowly and then burst into laughter. "Tea? Tea won't cure insanity, love!"

Mary tilted her head and clucked her tongue. "My poor Harold. Finally lost it."

"You're right, Mary. I have lost it. I've lost the love of my job. That's what I've been trying to tell you..."

"Didn't your mother start collecting red marbles when she went crazy, love?" Mary said.

"Yes, but..."

"What happened to them after she died?"

"Lost 'em in the move, I think... But who cares? I'm trying to say..."

"Lost the marbles? Oh, that's delightful," Mary said, a true smile spring-boarding onto her face. "Devilishly ironic and cliché."

"Cliché?" Harold asked.

"It's a technical English term, love. Never mind about it. It's irrelevant now that you're insane."

"Mary."

"Harold."

"I'm not crazy..."

"Of course you're not."

"I'm not!"

The tea kettle whistled in time to Harold slapping his hand on the table.

"Tea's almost ready!" Mary said. She poured them each a cup of the hot water and steeped the lemon tea bags. She carefully mixed in a tablespoon of honey and presented Harold with his own porcelain cup, and she sat down with hers. "There, isn't that nice?"

"Mary, listen to me."

"Of course, love."

"I'm quitting my job because I've been offered the Director of Marketing position at Saks."

"Saks?" Mary's eyes glazed.

They stared at each other with an equally-weighted look of pained understanding. Harold began nodding slowly.

"Saks. And it pays a whole helluva lot more than Holstein and Lowry did." Harold stood up. "Thanks for the tea," he said as he headed out of the room.

Mary sat at the table, stunned, repeating *Saks* over and over. Her ears closed dumbly to the sound of Harold laughing in the hallway. She stared at her half-completed crossword puzzle. *15 Down: Shakespearean tragedy with a king and a fool*.

"That's easy... *King Lear*," Mary murmured. She picked up her pencil and scribbled the answer. She stared at her own handwriting and murmured, "Saks." After a moment, Harold stuck his head back in the kitchen doorway. "You thought I'd just up and quit my job... Crazy..."

Mary's smile quivered. "I wasn't fooled for a second, love."

Written in circa 2000

Day Drinking

So a wookie, a dragon, and Bigfoot walk into a bar, see? And there's hardly anyone there because it's still early and the bartender's this old fucker who can barely make out his own wife anymore so he just thinks they're hippies or homeless people, which are really the only kind who'd be in the bar in the middle of the afternoon anyway, right? The dragon's the only one who can really say much that humans might understand as English, so he goes up to the bartender and orders a round for him and the boys. The bartender kinda grunts at him and mutters something about them not skipping out on their tab and the dragon's like, "Hey, mister, no problem, here's a brick of gold." A real brick of gold, ya know? So the bartender's trying to figure out what the hell this odd lookin' fella's giving him and he goes, "I don't get paid with rocks, son, you'll need to cough up some cash." The dragon kinda rolls his eyes, leaves the gold, and he and the wookie and Bigfoot all grab their drinks and go sit at a table. Bigfoot's antsy about playing darts and so he and the wookie get over there and start doing their thing while the dragon just guzzles the shit out of his beer, right? Then Bigfoot's jam, you know, the Katy Perry song "Hot and Cold," comes on the jukebox or whatever and he starts bopping around and chucks a dart wayward-like and it clips the wookie who's standing a little too close to the board for some reason and the dragon has to jump in between them to keep them from ripping each others fur out. Crazy shit. Meanwhile, the bartender's still fuming behind the taps because he thinks this hippie sonovabitch just ripped him off, right? And not just that, but he and his hoodlum friends are still lollygagging about and being noisy about it to boot. So he says to the one other guy sitting at the bar, "Hey, did you see that asshole stiff me on the tab?" and the other guy shrugs and goes, "No, but I did see what it was like to be drunk at the end of a rainbow."

Written in 2013

Guided Hypnosis #25

You unpack the last box and that's when your eye drifts to the disheveled book shelf and you search for your copy of *The Electric Kool-Aid Acid Test*, even though it can't be there. You let her borrow it in a past life with a note taped to the inside cover giving her permission to borrow this sacred copy of yours for up to ten years and you signed your name, solemnly and without humor. You meant it -- you wanted to give her all the time she'd need to flip through the pages, heavily annotated by you, different colors of ink underlining and commenting and circling things that struck you as you read them the first, second, third time. *You'll like it*, you'd told her as you shoved the book in her hands. *Trust me.* She'd looked at you with lukewarm eyes and said, *I do,* before setting it down and returning to the kitchen to pour some more whiskey.

You'd forgotten about this long-ago exchange until now as you unpack what was recently packed to transport you to a fresh, clean chapter with no underlines, comments, or circles yet on the page. You crouch, you squint, you lean back. You time travel back to that heartfelt day where you tried to share something meaningful with a person who was meaningful. How long ago was it, now? You press your fingers over your mouth as you concentrate. Three years? *Seven more to go*, you murmur out loud as you stand into your legs and survey the books that did come along for the journey. There's books by Kurt Vonnegut and Malcolm Gladwell and Lorrie Moore. There's biographies and books about war and books full of your annotations and books that have yet to be opened. But all you can think is *why the* fuck *did you let her borrow that particular book?* It was like giving her an entirely filled out journal from some point in your history. You hang your head and shake it. You've been wrong before this.

She was someone who floated alongside you for a period of time and it brought you a new brand of joy that took a strange turn. What you first read as *carefree* you later learned was total apathy; what you first read as *adventurous* you later learned was a slightly suicidal tendency; what you first read as *love* you later learned was manipulation. Yes, you've been wrong before this.

Yet, still, you wonder -- *Where's her heart now?* Yours is beating in your chest, just like always. You're curious about hers, though. You're curious where in time and space hers might be.

Once, she'd told you stories about her father. It was late at night and she was a grey shade of drunk and she'd leaned against you hard and told you about the time her mother was killed in a fire. *She could have gotten out*, she said with no inflection. *I got out, my dad got out -- she could have. But she didn't. And so she died. After that, my dad didn't know what to do -- with me, with himself, with life without her.* You wanted to interject with questions or support or anything to be more than just the wall she heaved her weight against, but you didn't want to break the spell, so you stayed perfectly still to see if there was more. And there was -- there were stories of her childhood, being carted from place to place by a father hellbent on chasing ghosts, on chasing death, on chasing anything that could get him out of this reality. Somewhere in the story, she paused and looked at you, really looked at you. *You understand*, she said and even though you weren't certain you did, you nodded, you let her go on.

It was nights like this that made you hand her your copy of *The Electric Kool-Aid Acid Test*. Something about the bus lifestyle, something about nicknames and synthetic realities, something about choosing your own family made you think of her. *You'll like it*, you'd told her as you shoved the book in her hands. *Trust me*. She'd looked at you with lukewarm eyes and said, *I do,* before setting it down and returning to the kitchen to pour some more whiskey.

There's still seven years to prove you wrong, but something tells you you're never getting that book back, the buzzing in your head a blaring dial tone with no one at the end of the line.

Written in 2015

Rolling Without Spinning

He said he bought it at an estate auction and she was too wide-eyed to ask more questions. "I'll call it the *Jam*bulance," he said giddily, pulling her around back to open the rear doors. She stared inside at the hollowed out husk of what had once been a carriage that saved lives and she blinked a smile. "Cool," she said, not that he was listening. One sideways glance showed that he was dreaming about his plans for this clunky, massive vehicle that still bore the gold streak of *make way for emergency* dashed across the exterior. "I can keep my amp over there and store my cases over there and these drawers will be great for all the cables," he said, hopping in and letting his imagination verbalize his every thought. "I've still got that velvet curtain and velvet ropes from the magic show," he added without looking back. She stayed on the ground and nodded in tandem with him.

Understandably, she didn't see him much for the next couple of weeks while he spilled all his blood, sweat, and tears into his new project. She still showed up for rehearsals and sang softly alone, never bothering to hit record or write a note. She'd remember what was good and the rest could fall away while she waited.

By the time he did answer one of her calls, it was the fourth ring and she'd already pursed her lips to adopt her Voicemail Tone, so she was startled to have him excitedly say, "We're ready to gig in the Jambulance -- get over here now!" She had no time to respond before he disconnected the call, so she went over to his apartment to find him in the parking lot with his monster truck.

"Look, it's beautiful," he said as she approached.

She wanted to find a flaw in his creation, anything to justify her desire to berate him for ignoring her and wasting time, but her eyes grew wide with abject curiosity as she moved without speaking towards the glowing beast.

"I've got a generator for the amps and stuff, but I figured we could do mostly acoustic to start," he said as she stared and stared at the twinkle lights he'd affixed to the velvet backdrop.

"This is... Wow," was all she could say.

"Let's take it for a spin," he said, ushering her to the passenger's side door before clanging the back shut and running around to the driver's side.

"Is this street legal?" she asked.

"Listen to that engine hum!" he ignored her.

She stared out the window.

He drove them a few blocks away to a frat house he'd been thrown out of many times and laid on the horn for a good thirty seconds until a couple of the guys came out. Boosting himself half out the window to yell over the top, "Check out the Jambulance!"

She sighed and got out on her side as he got out on his.

"What's this, bro?" one of the more articulate boys asked.

"Jambulance, I already said," he said with a hefty eye roll. "Look," he added, throwing the back doors open to reveal their mobile concert hall.

"Holy shit," said anyone else as he picked up a guitar and started playing a song she'd be unable to ignore.

It didn't take long for everyone on campus to hear about the Jambulance and, like a rock-and-roll Pied Piper, coeds flocked to wherever it was parked. She'd sit sometimes with her legs dangling off the back and let her hair fall across her face while he sang and she strummed. She'd only wince visibly when he'd try to work in a card trick, *for old time's sake*. More than anything, she wanted to be mad at him for making this mockery of everything she believed in with music. She wanted this scheme to be a total failure so they could go back to playing simple gigs at coffee shops and bars. And more than that, she wanted to squash the bubble of happiness she felt whenever someone would spot them parking and yell out, "It's here!" When the campus newspaper came to interview them one day, she let him do all the talking.

Then came the morning when she woke up sweating heavily from a nightmare. In it, the souls who'd lived and died in the place she now administered musical healing came and gathered at her feet as they swung off the back of the Jambulance. One small ghostly child grabbed at her shoe and giggled while an old man shook with tears just outside of her peripheral view. Awake now and afraid, she reached for the journal she always kept bedside and wrote

No spin to this sin,
this roll in the hey-
day of the way to save
what lives remain
in the aftermath

of emergency -- sirens
blare in the blood-
soaked stare
of eyes that won't roll
no more -- no more
running these red
lights, no more strumming
to break up fights,
no more spin to this sin
this roll in the hey-
day of the wave to save
what lives remain
in the aftermath
of emergency --

and when she was done writing that, she heard its melody, too, and so she got up and got dressed and got out of her dorm room to unlock the Jambulance and take it for a solo joyride up the coast. He never let her drive, but he'd given her the spare keys, if only because irresponsibility made him likely to lock them both out. She rolled the window down and dropped her elbow outside as she cruised through the early morningness of the moment. Somewhere near the water, she parked and got out and threw open the back doors to find him, dazed and disheveled in the tousle.

"What are we doing here?" he asked her through blinks and jaw clicks while a frightened, half-naked blonde huddled somewhere behind him.

She eyed them coolly and with restraint. "I meant to come alone," was all she said before walking with her hand shoved deeply into her pockets right down to the water's edge.

He jogged after her, sheepish and without apology. "We had a good jam sesh, if you know what I mean," he said as he nudged her side.

"You know I don't care about that," she said, making a mental note of the colors the sun turned the water as it rose.

"What were you going to do here alone?" he asked.

At this, she turned hard to look at him. "We'll never know," she said.

"What are we going to do now here together?" he asked.

She sighed and looked at the ground. "Break up," she said.

"But why?" he asked.

She looked at him softly. "You're on a roll but I'm just on a spin," she said. "We're out of time." With that, she handed him back the spare set of keys and walked back up towards the road, edging away from their traveling carnival act with the grace of a peripheral ghost.

Written in 2018

Arrivals and Departures

"It just gets hard to believe
that god sent this angel to watch over me
cuz my angel -- she don't receive my calls
She says I'm too dumb to fuck
Too dumb to fight
Too dumb to save
Well, maybe I don't need no angel at all --"
~ Counting Crows

He missed his flight on purpose again. Sitting in the Miami International Airport outside the security checkpoint, he stared at the screens flashing *Departed* and rubbed his hands together. Somewhere in his bag was his phone. He would call Lucy and have her come back to get him. He'd stay here another day or two. He'd stay here indefinitely if he had to.

His backpack was grey and dirty and starting to rip at the shoulder straps. Inside, he had three pairs of dirty underwear, two t-shirts -- one that said "I Pooped Today" and another that had a cartoon banana on it -- a pair of green cargo shorts and seven knotted bandanas. Lucy had teased him about the bandanas, pointing out that he could convert them into underwear -- she'd seen a stripper do it at the club where she worked as a cocktail waitress -- and she'd taken her time showing him how. He smiled a little, thinking about Lucy. She was pretty when you looked at her quickly -- all white teeth and tan skin and frantically curly long brown hair. It was only when you looked at her longer that you saw the weariness in her eyes, the desperation to be happy with what she was doing. That's what attracted him to her -- the desperation. His soul suctioned to that. His mind clamped around it.

They'd met at a bar in Boston where she was working for the summer. He played the guitar in a cover band that frequently landed on her stage and they'd bonded over their attraction to cheap whiskey and Creedence Clearwater Revival. He'd play her "Have You Ever Seen the Rain?" and she'd tolerate him climbing on top of her in the apartment she was subletting from an old college friend. Both of them were too old to be living like they were which only made them drink more, fuck more, go on more mind erasing benders for days at a time, rolling on the grass in the Public Garden while tourists tried to take nice family photos with the swan boats as a backdrop. If they could ruin the moment, they would, and when that summer ended and Lucy had to head back to Florida, it had felt like spiders crawling through his gut. It only took a week before he bought a ticket and went to visit her. He told everyone it was love.

Sitting in the airport, he fished around and found his phone in his backpack's front pocket and grimaced at the low battery level. He'd left his charger plugged in behind a row of open cereal boxes at Lucy's current sublet. He knew he should call her right away and see when she could come and get him, but he also wondered if he should just get on the next flight and return home.

Stop being such a child, a familiar voice cracked through his skull. *Get your ass on the plane. The real world won't stop just because you wish it would.*

He swallowed hard and stared at the phone, wondering if *hers* was the number he should be dialing. It had been a long time since he'd dared and even the thought of seeing her name on the screen, the tiny round picture of her happy face in the upper left hand corner, made him feel immediately nauseous. She'd never take his call. He would never hear her voice out loud ever again.

Yet, still, she echoed through his brain every day, without fail.

"Amy, I'm sorry," he muttered out loud before glancing sharply left and right to see if anyone heard him. But the world simply spun madly by.

Amy was the sister of his former fiance Jane. Jane was his high school sweetheart and they'd rediscovered each other right after college only to realize they were more in love than ever, but three days after their engagement, she'd fallen ill and passed away suddenly. It was a tragedy by all measurable standards -- but the one silver lining to this dark, black cloud was the bond that formed between Amy and him. The next seven years, their friendship defined both of their lives. They depended on each other, they loved each other, they grieved the loss of Jane together and healed and moved on together. He liked being around her -- she reminded him of his lost love in a way that was comforting. She seemed to like being around him because he'd had access to a version of her sister that she'd never really known. They were good for each other.

As time marched on, though, Amy's career advanced, she stopped pulling all-nighters at bars and stopped coming to all of his shows. They still talked every day, but he could feel her drifting and it panicked him --

especially when she started dating a new man who was his polar opposite: career-driven, successful, clean. One night, he convinced her to meet him for drinks alone and he was nervous so he drank too much and in his sloppiness, he'd leaned in to kiss her, saying, "Please, come home with me tonight." She'd pushed back from him, a look of disgusted confusion on her face, and said an even, "No." But he'd tried again, this time grabbing the back of her neck and pulling her to him. "You're my angel," he slurred, his eyes glassy. "You watch over me. You take care of me in ways I can't explain. All I want is to take care of you." She yanked herself out of his grip and calmly stood up. "I don't need you to take care of me." And she left.

After that, they spoke less and less -- and it was always her politely accepting every third call from him. During this time, he deteriorated more and more. His casual state of being unkempt escalated aggressively, as did his state of anti-sobriety. This was when her voice began to swirl through his brain like a tornado -- criticizing, correcting, commanding. His imagination took flight and with it, his resentment of her, both for the rejection he felt and the goading he'd crafted in her likeness. All of this came to a head at her thirtieth birthday party, held at a bar where his band was playing, and he'd tried hard to pull himself together -- to shower and shave and dress like he wasn't a seventeen-year-old -- his intentions were good. But as the night went on and she paid little attention to him and the band, instead hanging out in the back of the bar with her boyfriend, he'd pounded shots of whiskey and then got on the microphone and said, "Happy birthday to my favorite cunt!" The room stood still as the speakers squeaked out some feedback and he'd stumbled backwards, tripping over his guitar pedal. "Cheers," he added, righting himself to get ready for the next song.

Amy's eyes had connected with his in that moment, and if he remembered nothing else clearly about what happened in those moments, it was the hurt she flashed before grabbing her jacket and slamming out into the night. He made it until the last song before he went into the bathroom to throw up in the sink.

He'd dialed her number so many times since then and she'd refused him every time. *I don't need you to take care of me, but you sure as shit need me to take care of you,* her voice rumbled through his head on a daily basis.

Sitting in the Miami International Airport, he tried to conjure Lucy's voice in his head, tried to make her his guardian angel, but all that yielded was static. He stared at the board of Arrivals and Departures as his phone went dead in his hands.

Written in 2015

Guided Hypnosis #17

Drip-drop.

This is what you hear on repeat while you sleep on the couch in your best friend Marla's apartment. It's Night #3 and what was previously drowned out by your broken-hearted tears is now starting to annoy you beyond all human reason.

Drip-drop.
Call landlord.
Drip-drop.
Call landlord.
Drip-drop.
Call landlord.

You get up and look for a wrench. It's three a.m. and everyone else is sleeping, especially the landlord who you couldn't call anyway since you don't actually live here. After tripping over Marla's boyfriend's gigantic flip flops and pausing for a moment for your usual daydream about what those huge feet must mean about the rest of him, you manage to kick them aside as you head into the kitchen to see if you can find any tools. Standing under the dull yellow light, you roll your eyes and add "Get better lighting" to your list of landlord demands before letting your head swivel around, owl-like, as you ask yourself the notorious three a.m. question: "If I were a wrench in Marla's apartment, this is where I'd be." You knew where the wrenches are at your own apartment, but you don't really live there anymore so you perk up immediately, deciding not to live in the past, and throw open the under sink doors to see what you find.

"Tiki torch oil?" you muse as you stare at the large plastic bottle of yellow-orange liquid. You look around the Medford, Massachusetts apartment, complete with no backyard or, as far as you know, tiki torches, and you shrug.

Despite the racket you're making as you knock over cans of WD-40 and bleach-filled all-purpose cleaners, all you hear is silence punctuated by *drip-drop.*

Make it stop, you start to rhyme in your head.

You start knocking things over in the kitchen, hoping Marla will become disturbed and maybe check on you. Surely, she knows where there's a wrench.

Drip-drop.

This leaky faucet is your nemesis now. You narrow your eyes and stomp into the bathroom. You press your hands into the pseudo-porcelain sink and you stare at the rusted metal fixture that has slowly driven you insane. There, from the sides, water eeks out, shamelessly, right in front of you.

Drip.

Drop.

Your rage deflates as you catch a glimpse of your tense and grimacing face in the mirror. Your cheeks are bright red and your teeth are ground together as your locked jaw juts out. You are a caricature of anger. How can *this* be you? Slumping to the tiled floor, you press a hand against your face and you laugh quietly. Only two nights ago, you'd sat in this exact same place with your body choking on tears and rage and betrayal. Only two nights ago, you were certain you could not go on. But here you are -- in the same spot with a different problem and the weight of that relief causes your head to drop squarely into your hands.

"Hey," a sleepy voice says from the doorway. "Hey, what are you doing?"

You look up and see Marla, confused and yawning.

"I heard a bunch of noise and I thought..." she goes on.

You offer her an apologetic smile and you nod towards the faucet. "It's leaky," you say.

Marla seems confused. "Oh," she says.

"I was going to try and fix it for you," you say. "But I couldn't find a wrench."

Marla comes over and slumps onto the floor beside you. "Do you know how to fix a leaky faucet?" she asks.

You shake your head. "I bet the internet does, though," you say.

Drip-drop.

"Make it stop," you whisper in a sing-song voice.

Marla smiles. "Look at you, turning this leaky faucet into a hip hop beat."

"Whole new career path for me: plumber rap star," you say weakly.

Marla slings an arm around your shoulder and your heads rest together. "You're going to be OK," she says resiliently. "And *this* is how I know it."

You look at her and let her surety convince you. "Do you have a wrench?" you ask hopefully.

Marla laughs. "I'll call the landlord in the morning."

"Or you could try this," her gigantic boyfriend says, coming out of nowhere to lean over you both and twist a washer on the faucet.

You all wait in silence for what seems like an eternity and only exhale your relief when you are convinced the nightmare has passed.

"Thanks, Dave," you both say as he helps you to your feet.

"Any time," he says as you stare at his gargantuan naked feet shuffling him back into the bedroom.

You and Marla stand there for a few moments longer before she yawns and leans in to give you a hug.

"Sleep well, my friend," she says.

"What kind of person has tiki torch oil but no wrench?" you ask, letting her go.

"The kind who knows how to have a good party," she says with a wink, walking away.

Your curl back up on the couch, relieved to hear nothing but silence as you shut your mind down for the night and fall asleep to dream about the good and the solvable. This is a step in the right direction.

Written in 2013

Don't Believe

"I don't believe in love anymore," he said. "It's all about sex."

She closed her eyes and said nothing. Even with her eyes closed, she could still see the shadow of brown hair on his newly shaved head, his wiry glasses sliding off the end of his petite nose, the gray in his eyes appearing violet in the shadow of the street light.

"I mean, love is like a postcard, vague and easily misinterpreted -- *wish you were here, the weather's nice*," he said. "Sex is real, physical, concrete -- I can feel it, touch it. I'm never conflicted about whether or not I've had it."

With her eyes closed, she could hear his nervous energy more distinctly, hear the tapping of his feet on the cement path, the jingling of some coins in his drooping pockets. She could hear him tapping his teeth together, the annoying click of chatter brought on by frustration rather than cold.

"I should have moved to Hawaii," he continued, "where all the hula girls straddle bar stools whether they're currently occupied or not."

She swallowed thickly as his nervous noises grew louder. She could hear the quick draw of his breath, the pant of hula pleasure. She could hear the unholy drag of his tongue across his pale lips, the way it rested on the corner as if to absorb the last bit of salt leftover from movie popcorn.

"Yeah, those hula girls can be pretty slutty." He laughed once, from his gut. "I remember sitting in this bar -- The Bunny Hop --" He laughed again and paused.

She knew he was waiting to see if she'd respond for once. She could feel the weight of his twenty-four-year-old stare where her opened eyes should be. She could feel his eyes narrow, concentrate their unrelenting gaze where her pupils would be if she'd open her lids.

"The Bunny Hop," he repeated, his voice louder. "A divey place if there ever was one. A lot of nice tits-n-ass, though. A very friendly population in Hawaii. And you know the old expression *they breed like rabbits*."

She turned her face to the side and tried not to clench her jaw. She knew he was clenching his jaw, the tension in his cheeks drawing veins to the surface of his neck, his ears turning red from cold and silence.

"Yeah, a lot of friendly hula girls at The Bunny Hop. It might have been a slummy place, but it felt enough like home. I mean, all slums feel the same, don't they? All shit hole bars smell alike and look alike....walk alike and talk alike... Don't they? All sluts fuck alike, too. Not like you, though. None of them knew quite enough tricks to beat your high score."

She folded her arms across her chest and listened to him shudder as a sharp gust of wind stung his face. She could hear him rocking on the soles of his weather-beaten tennis shoes. She could hear him shove his hands in his pockets and jingle the coins again. She could hear him clear his dry throat.

"No, none of them are you. Hula girls or mainland chicks. None of them make me feel as alive as you did. Damn, I'm so tired -- of missing you. But, fuck it. I'm really just talking."

She turned her face towards the ground. Her hair swung over her cheeks, and she thought again about his naked head. Buzzed. He must be cold, and she knew he hated being cold. He must be wishing he'd waited until spring. He must have been absent in school the day the teacher said *heat escapes fastest through your head* and when she'd added, *you could stand outside with nothing on but a hat and be surprisingly warm*. This from the same teacher who, on Halloween, wore a long, pale blond wig made with the hair from her dead mother. Of course, third grade was a long time ago, and maybe he'd had a different kind of teacher than she had. But he must be cold, he must. Regardless of who he'd had in third grade.

"I'm just talking," he repeated, louder. "I'm here with you, after all, not in Hawaii. Here, this close, practically on top of you, and missing you more than ever. Hell, I don't care about The Bunny Hop or hula girls. I'm telling you about them as a *for instance* -- because they do just fine without love. Love's a Hallmark Holiday." He spit. "And I don't really care that you're not talking to me tonight." He paused, cracked his jaw. "I don't need to think I love you anymore."

Without opening her eyes, her head jerked up, and she inhaled deeply. She listened to him exhale his disgust and turn and walk away. She listened to him clear his throat as he slapped the rubber soles of his shoes methodically on the cement path. She listened to him roll his shoulders, flare his nostrils, and forget about his instinctive need to cry. She fought back the urge to stop him, to yell, *"It* is *about love! It* is *about warmth! It* is *about caring and chances and you need me as much as I need you!"* But she didn't. She knew him well enough to wait until he was gone before she allowed herself to cry.

And she opened her invisible eyes. The wind stung around her as she swung her gaze towards the ground. He had dropped a bright red rosebud near her. Kneeling, she touched the damp grass beside the silky flower, wondered if he knew she saw him best with her eyes closed, saw him best outside of her body. Her tears fell fast on the ground as she steadied herself on the square headstone she guarded, her own, the barrier between his banishment of love and her exile from life. She rubbed her fingers over the last worldly reminder that she had lived twenty-one years, died twenty-one years into her allotted time on the planet, and told herself to hold steady to the stone, hold steady to life. It wasn't time to let go. He still needed her; she still believed in love and didn't believe in any form of absolute death. *Don't believe it's over*, she thought with her eyes fixed on the rosebud.

Written in circa 2000

The Player Piano

Dried blood, faded and brown, splattered the keys on the player piano. Marcus sat on the swivel stool with a bowl of stale Cheerios and popped the milkless cereal bits into his mouth one at a time as he stared at the layer of dust that covered the stains on the once-white keys.

"Think anyone misses the dead guy?" his brother Louis said from behind.

Marcus shrugged. "Wonder if this old thing still works." He squinted his eyes in the dull light and then reached over to flip the switch. Nothing happened, so Marcus stood up. "We should go," he said, crunching on a piece of Cheerio.

"We didn't look for Grandpa's box yet," Louis said, not moving.

Marcus set his plastic bowl down and sighed. "Fine, OK," he said.

The brothers started moving boxes and looking under covered furniture and even lifted the lid on the player piano but after twenty minutes, nothing had turned up.

"Satisfied?" Marcus asked Louis.

Louis' eyes settled back on the stained keys. "Yeah," he said.

"Wild goose chase over?" Marcus asked Louis.

Louis didn't even blink. "Yeah," he said.

Marcus picked up his bowl of Cheerios again and snacked for a thoughtful moment. "We should burn this place," he said.

"Yeah," Louis said, still transfixed.

Marcus put a hand on his brother's shoulder and yanked him out of his daze. "Ain't nothing to remember about the dead," he said. "Ain't no difference how gone people get gone."

"Yeah," Louis said, walking over and closing the cover over the keys, burying the sight of old blood from their view. Tapping his knuckle on the wood, he turned to face his brother and began to nod. "We're like this player piano, you know?" he asked.

Marcus crunched. "How's that?"

"We operate in a loop with pre-programmed material no matter what goes on around us, no matter what we witness, no matter what happens, and then one day we don't work anymore," Louis said.

Marcus set his cereal down, brushed off his hands, and said, "Yeah." After a pause, he added, "Come on, let's go."

"I bet someone misses the dead guy," Louis said as he lingered a moment.

"Grandpa's box is probably buried outside," Marcus said, ignoring him. "In the woods somewhere. We'll never find it."

"Yeah," Louis said. "Probably just has some old reels for this player piano anyway."

Marcus didn't need to withdraw the shakily handwritten letter in his back pocket from his now-dead grandfather to see the words *Family legacy's in there -- you gotta find it* scrolling through his mind's eye. "Maybe," Marcus said. "Let's just forget it and go."

The two men shuffled their way out of the dusty cabin and back to the truck parked at a slant outside.

"What about the fire?" Louis said as Marcus revved the engine.

Marcus sighed. "Wait here," he said, hopping out of the truck and heading back in the cabin. Withdrawing a lighter from his pocket, he flicked out a flame and watched it dance close to his face for a moment while his eyes focused on the dead instrument against the wall. Crouching down, he touched the edge of the flame to a smelly wool blanket tossed over a wooden crate and watched as smoke and fire started to eat away at these man made things.

"Let's go then," said Louis from the doorway.

Marcus shifted his gaze over his shoulder and sniffed. "How many bodies you think are buried here?"

Louis shrugged. "Doesn't matter anymore."

Marcus stood up and walked past his brother to the truck. "Yeah," he said as they both climbed into the vehicle.

Thick curls of smoke were visible from the road long after they pulled away from the scene, neither of the men talking or joking or making music of any kind for miles and miles.

Written in 2013

Guided Hypnosis #27

Sometimes it takes a psychic to slap you in the face with your poor life choices. Hunched on a red couch a man had to assemble for you, you sigh as this woman you've met only twice in your life gives you the same advice she'd given on the previous occasions: *be done, move past, let go*. Somewhere nearby there is surely some orange juice being overwhelmed with vodka and ready to be downed by you. Somewhere nearby there is surely an escape hatch out of this life. Either way, you let the verbal beating continue as you think about the words of the great Albert Einstein: *Insanity: doing the same thing over and over and expecting different results*. You, according to Uncle Al, are insane. That is what the psychic is telling you.

She says other things, too, things that are positive and renewing, things that confirm you are otherwise on the right path. She has words of praise and positivity. She knows you will be a success and she tells you your grandfather is the one watching over you from above. You feel these things in your heart before she says them and there is relief in all of that.

But it's short lived when all you take away is how wrong you are about love. She tells you that you don't value yourself. She tells you that you have trouble letting people take care of you. She tells you that you invest in the wrong people and that a love more real and powerful than you've ever known will come as soon as you learn to value yourself and let someone in to take care of you and get rid of bad investments. She tells you happiness is yours for the taking but only if you make some changes.

You thank her for her time. You hang up the phone.

You sit and you stare at the wall in total silence. You barely even blink.

Later, you will pour your heart out to one sister after another, an endless stream of powerful women who've loved and lost and learned, just like you, and they will offer advice based on what they know. You will thank them. You will go home alone.

Later, you will try to sort this mess out yourself. You will write a letter, you will cry. You will paint your fingernails the color of enlightenment without cutting off the obvious hangnail. You will put on the brightest yoga gear you own and you will get on your mat. You will try to assess what sort of value you really have and, despite everything you have seen and heard (or maybe because of it) you will be unsure that you have any at all.

But before you can even get off that red couch, you will let the psychic's words bounce through your brain -- *It's like being an alcoholic and needing another drink. Don't take another drink.* Maybe you're waiting for rock bottom. You're undoubtedly waiting for something as you stare and stare and stare.

Written in 2013

The Old Stone Church

Once there was a girl who lived in a house by a hill. At the top of the hill was an old stone church with one tall tree standing by it. She could see the tall tree by the old stone church on top of the hill from her bedroom window and she liked to imagine climbing all the way to the top. She never left her room, so she never knew what it was like to feel the wind against her face from the highest limb. But she could imagine.

The girl had a younger brother who was more often outside than inside. She would watch him run all over the lawn, sometimes up the hill towards the tree by the old stone church, but he never went all the way to it. She sometimes wondered why he steered clear of it but she never asked.

She almost never spoke to her brother anymore.

Instead, she stayed in her pink and yellow room and thought about what everyone outside was doing. Sometimes she daydreamed about real people and sometimes imagined. She would give them funny names like Candice Stiltpepper and Hawthorne McGuyver. Sometimes she would even rename people she knew -- like Mrs. Sneed would become Mrs. Sneezykerchief. All this imagining filled her head and filled her days so much that she sometimes forgot to eat or go to bed on time after properly saying her prayers. It didn't matter much to her, though, because she was just so happy -- truly happy.

Her little brother was like a puppy who wanted to follow her around but was too restless to stay indoors all the time. But he figured out how much she liked to pretend because he would come back in from his day's adventure and feed her information about the outside world..

"The house two doors down is blue," he said because she'd never seen it.

Later that day, she'd see his shadow under her door and she'd tell a story out loud about a blue house with brown shutters and a chimney made of pepper shakers that rattled on windy days but Mr. and Mrs. Bowden Forceland hadn't minded because the master of the house sold insurance for just such architectural oddities. Her brother's shadow slipped away as she moved into a description of what the Forcelands were eating for lunch. Never mind, though, her imagination was already spinning with ideas about the blue house. She'd remain occupied with them for a long time.

For this reason, she loved the bits of information her brother would tell her. It was the only way she learned about what was beyond her own window view. She just had no desire to leave and see more on her own. And there was no need with such a great scout.

One day, she was deep in a daydream about Merry Weatherspoon and Louis von Greenhow when she saw her brother creep up the hill toward the tree by the old stone church. Her eyes first grew wide and then narrowed to slits as she forgot about Merry and Louis' impending trip to the grocery store and, instead, she focused all of her attention on her brother. He drew closer and closer to her tree by the old stone church. But when he was close enough to touch it, he instead backed down completely, looking around as if he'd trespassed. She watched as he scampered back down the hill and towards the house. She sat silently for a long time, staring at the tree, waiting for him to come and visit her. She needed to know what he'd been doing.

She waited for more than an hour before she heard his footsteps in the hall and for what seemed like an eternity for his hands to wrap around the door and push it open. Then there he was, finally, in her room.

"Tell me about the tree," she said quietly.

Her brother seemed startled -- it had been so long since she spoke *to* him, after all. His mouth hung agape for a few silent moments before she asked again:

"Tell me about the tree."

He stood with his back pressed against the wall, his hands folded neatly in front of him.

"I'm not allowed near the tree," he said.

"Why not?" she asked.

"Mother and Dad said."

She leaned forward. "Why?"

He shrugged evasively. "Dunno."

"Liar," she said sharply and he slouched a little. "I saw you near it today," she went on.

"I was just goofin' around," he said.

"That's my tree," she hissed. "Mine!"

The little boy couldn't back any more into the wall, but he tried anyway. "I'm sorry," he said.

She continued to glare but felt her will soften when she saw how afraid of her he was.

"I want to know about that tree," she said, her features relaxing. "Find out everything there is to know."

The boy seemed to take this as his cue to escape, so he nodded and fled the room. She moved quickly to her window to see him do her bidding but minutes and hours passed without any sign of him. In fact, she did not see even a hint of her brother for nearly four days. And as those minutes and hours and days passed, she felt her imagination weakening under the strain of this vigilant watch. She didn't create new stories -- she couldn't. She needed to know about that tree by the old stone church.

And then -- finally -- she saw her brother outdoors once more. But he did not go near her tree. Later that day, he came and stood outside her closed door and said, "I saw a lady with a large green straw hat."

A wave of gratitude washed over her and she began crafting a story about Mrs. Lavender Daffodil and her new hat, a gift from her son, an important senator in the United States Senate. As she built up the story, she heard her brother's footsteps walk away.

They did not discuss the tree again for days, even though she kept a watchful eye on it, hoping to know what story would be special enough to tell about her favorite thing in the whole wide world.

Then one morning, she saw her brother's shadow outside her door and saw the knob turn. Entering her room, he had an arm bent behind his back, concealing something.

"Happy birthday," he said.

She blinked. Was it her birthday? She hadn't realized. "What's that?" she asked, pointing at his bent arm.

He shifted. "A birthday present." And he stretched out his arm to offer a small brown diary. She stood stock still so he laid it on her bed. "It's Mother's. I'll need it back," he said as he slipped out of the room.

She picked up the journal and sat in her chair by the window that looked out on the tree by the old stone church. Opening the diary, she saw a marker tucked into a page in the middle. Without giving it a second thought, she flipped to that page and read her mother's neat cursive writing.

October 26th

Caught Lillian in her room talking to her imaginary friend again. Brother, she calls him. Telling stories to thin air about the neighbors. Doesn't even have the decency to pretend she's talking to her stuffed bears. Oh, what a child. "You know I always wanted a brother, Mummy," she says to me. If only I could provide one for her, I would.

October 30th

Today, Lillian insisted we allow her to try again to climb that tree. You'd think she'd learn her lesson after that nasty spill she took the last time. But you know Lillian, once she gets an idea in her head... I, of course, said no, but her father can deny her nothing, so he promised after supper they'd walk up there. I won't go near that abandoned old church -- it gives me the creeps.

October 31st

Oh, my Lillian, I'm so sorry I didn't believe you.

It was the last entry in the diary.

The girl sat with the brown diary in her hands and didn't know what to do. What did it mean? She was the child -- Lillian. That was her tree. Looking towards it now, she saw her brother sitting on a low branch, his legs swinging back and forth. Without thinking, the girl got up and walked out of her room, down the hall to the stairs and out the front door. My, the house was so dark!

Outside, she was stunned for a moment by the clarity of a drawn breath in fresh air and the green of the grass without the layer of glass in between but her mission moved her forward and she ran as fast as her legs could carry her up the hill to the tree by the old stone church. Winded, she stood and looked up at the dangling legs of her brother.

"You used to tell Mother I was real and you were right to do so," he said.

"Well, of course!" she said.

"Mother never believed in me. Dad neither. But you always did and that made me feel special."

The girl watched her brother's legs swing back and forth. "What do you mean Mother never believed..."

"I was the one who told you to climb this tree, you know." Her brother's face tilted down to face hers. "*That day.* It was me."

"What day? I've never been to this tree before. What do you mean?"

"Why, of course you've been here before. Didn't you read the diary? I marked the page."

"Yes, I read it. But I didn't understand it at all. I've never been to this tree. And I have a brother. Mother wrote that you weren't real, that I'd imagined you. But you're real. And I've never climbed this tree."

"Oh, but my sister, you have."

The girl suddenly felt cold and drew her arms tightly around herself. "You're scaring me."

"No reason to be scared. The scary part's over. The scary part was climbing this tree like I did when I was an altar boy at the old stone church. I wasn't supposed to climb it, but I did when I sneaked out during a Sunday service on Halloween. I wanted to climb that tree and scoot over near a window and tap on it during the sermon and give everyone inside a little spook. But the branch broke and I fell and I broke my neck." The boy smiled kindly at her. "I didn't get to scare them like I wanted."

The girl put a protective hand against her own neck. "Stop scaring me," she said.

"Lillian, *my sister*, I wanted you to help me scare them! That's why I came to you. That's why I asked you to beg your parents to let you climb this tree. And the first time you did, you were so close to following my instructions to the letter -- but you didn't climb high enough and you couldn't reach the window before the branch broke. You only sprained your ankle, though, so it wasn't too bad. It wasn't hard for me to convince you to try it again. You were scared, but you were ready to help your brother do anything. I couldn't ask for a better sister."

The girl stared silently at him.

"Come up here with me, sister," he said, extending his hand. She hesitated for a moment and then allowed him to help her up next to him. "I was there the last time you spoke to your mother," he said quietly. "You told her your brother needed your help. You told her where to find the article about my fall, but she thought it was your overactive imagination on a sunny Halloween day. No one had used this church for so long and the story about me was long forgotten. Your mother was in the house, in your room, looking up here at the tree as your father helped boost you up to where we are right now and then you climbed higher than you did the first time and when the branch snapped and you fell from that great height, it was all over so fast." He paused and took her hand in his. "You didn't even get to shimmy over near the window. You didn't do it like I told you to."

The girl tore her gaze away from the boy's face and looked down the hill towards her house. There were no lights on and the backyard was ripe with weeds. From her place in the tree by the old stone church, she could see no living soul.

* author's note: this story started out as something to do while I waited for Tom, Nate, Adam, and Tom to finish up their sound check at The Stone Church, Halloween 2009.

Spin

Molly heard the clatter and knew that Spin must be up to no good. Sighing, she got up from her desk chair and padded in socked feet over to the kitchen. Sure enough, her boyfriend Todd's tiny black and tan dachshund stood by his overturned water bowl looking up at her as if to say, "What are *you* gonna do about it?" She could feel the toe of her socks starting to saturate.

"Great" she muttered, bending down to pick the bowl up.

Spin followed her over to the sink while she filled it back up and returned it to its spot on a plastic food mat that had once belonged to her niece Jade. "At least she learned to clean up after herself," Molly said pointedly at the dog, whose tiny nails tapped in time as he followed her back down the hallway to the room she'd claimed as her home office. As she sat back in her chair, Spin nosed his way under a blanket that she'd left on the floor for moments such as these. She knew he'd burrow under there, his black eyes shining out from under the soft fleece, his thin red collar slid in such a way as to expose his heart-shaped dog tag that read *Got lost lookin' for bitches. Please call my human* with Todd's cell phone number on the back.

"It was a gift," Todd had said with a shrug when Molly had seen it for the first time.

"My inner feminist cries out in protest," she'd said, giving him a disdainful look.

When they stood next to each other, Todd towered over Molly by almost a full foot, but when they were lying next to each other on the couch, they always felt perfectly matched.   Cuddled together in that moment, Todd had pulled playfully on her ear and said, "I don't want your inner feminist to cry."

Catching a glimpse of the tag now, Molly nearly shivered at the memory of the delightful progression that had landed her fully satisfied, inner feminist and all. That's how Todd usually deflected from her politics, her stance on *things* -- he'd woo her. He'd delight her. He'd echo her words back at her in a way that clearly evidenced he didn't understand her brain but he knew *exactly* how to please her body.

As Spin's eyes closed, giving way to a nap-in-progress, Molly turned back to her computer screen and stared at the words she'd typed just before she'd heard the sound of the dog's flippant need for attention.

...what, then, to make of bell hooks' claim that it is "often easier to ignore, dismiss, reject, and even hurt one another rather than engage in constructive confrontation."

"Hell if I know," Molly said.

Spin curled into a ball behind her.

Molly was an adjunct professor of English Literature at Gaites Community College where she taught two classes: American Literature and Contemporary Literature. Neither of these class titles inspired any sort of imagination or passion within her, but she was allowed to develop her own curriculum, so she worked hard to mix in some writers of color, women writers, women writers of color... She didn't get the sense that most of her students understood the effort or why she was making it, but she kept on trying to teach them, anyway.

What she *really* wanted to be doing was working on her PhD -- she wanted to be a tenure-track professor at an accredited college or university -- not teaching twice a week and bartending five shifts at Jimmy's. She tried to comfort herself in that she'd met Todd during one of those bartending shifts at Jimmy's and that kissing him in the rain at two a.m. the night they met while he drunkenly -- if not sweetly -- tugged on her ear was one of the most vivid memories of her entire life. He'd come back the next night and the one after that and the one after that, finally seducing her in the back seat of his car while she was on a break there on Day Number Four.

"My last name is Jorgeson," he told her as she put her shirt back on.

They'd started dating in a more official capacity after about three months of fooling around at Jimmy's and when Todd took her out on their first official date, she felt almost uncomfortable climbing into the front seat of his car.

"You vacuumed in here or something," she said to reduce her own anxiety.

He leaned over and kissed her on the cheek. "You haven't seen nothin' yet," he promised.

That night, he brought her back to his apartment where he lived alone, except for Spin, who barked ferociously the minute she walked through the door.

"This is Spin. He's sweet, once you get to know him," Todd said with a wry smile as he scooped his dog up and pecked his head with noisy kisses.

Molly liked to see this big man adore this tiny animal. It made her feel safe. It made her put a soft hand on his arm. "Why don't you give me the tour?" she asked.

Todd set Spin down. "Yeah, sure," he said, eventually shooing his dog into the hallway as he closed the bedroom door for the night.

When Molly moved in about five months later, that's when she started to wonder if maybe the dog was still mad at her for gently distracting his owner ever since that first night. Certainly, they never were successful in shutting him out of the bedroom for more than a few minutes before he started whining and scratching to be let in. He peed on Molly's shoes -- once *without* her realizing it, which made for a soggy surprise -- and never one time hopped up on her lap, like he always did with Todd. One time while the three of them lazed on the couch and Spin gave Molly what she could only term as "the evil eye," she'd wondered out loud, "Who gave you his tag?"

"What, babe?" Todd asked, simultaneously stroking Spin's head and rubbing the back of her neck.

"His tag. The one that says he's off meeting bitches. You told me once it was a gift," Molly said.

Todd chuckled. "Says he got *lost* meeting bitches," he corrected. "Yeah, it was a gift. So what?"

"Who gave it to you?" she asked.

Todd shifted. "Why do you ask?"

"I'm just curious," she said.

"This girl Amanda," he said.

Molly bit her bottom lip. "Well, I guess that explains why he hates me so much," she said.

"What do you mean?" Todd asked.

"Did he like Amanda?" Molly asked.

"Babe," Todd said, sitting straight up. "Amanda's a friend."

"I'm sure," Molly said. "Never mind. Forget I asked."

Todd stared at her for a lingering moment before relaxing back into the couch. "What do you mean, Spin adores you," he said.

Molly said nothing as the dog curled his lips in a silent snarl.

She'd lived in Todd's apartment for three years now and things never exactly warmed up between Spin and her. For awhile, she'd tried -- she'd buy him special treats and toys, she'd coo and make a big fuss over him, she'd take him for long walks to dog parks where she knew he had "friends." But the truth was she wasn't a dog-person and Spin knew it. She could feel him judging her "white lady-ness," trying to advocate for minority cultures while attempting to masquerade as a minority for her femaleness. She could feel his indignation at her arrogance, her undue self-aggrandizing for all of the "work" she was doing for "others." She was a feminist fraud and this dog knew it.

She called other women bitches, for chrissakes. She'd done it in a text not twenty minutes ago sent to one of her co-workers at the bar. And she'd used it to call another woman *a bitch*. What kind of lie was she living that she'd get haughty about her boyfriend's dog wearing that ugly word around his neck? Spin understood too much about her. He'd looked too deeply into her eyes. He *knew her*.

Sitting in her desk chair, staring at the words of bell hooks, wondering if she would ever finish this essay, anyway, and submit it for peer review, she looked back at the dog, now snoring lightly from under the blanket.

"You spilled that water on purpose," she said, snapping shut her laptop and heading into the bathroom to put on lipstick to get ready for her next shift.

Written in 2020

Guided Hypnosis #3

You won't really want to go. You're tired and you're drunk and it's been a long day. But there are only five of you left now and everyone else wants to make one more stop: pizza! You can make it one more stop. Someone calls out a parlor in another neighborhood so you will all hop into cabs to take you there. You will end up in a cab with a man you think of as a close friend. You will have to tell the cab driver where to go – your friend will be too drunk to say much.

As the cab drives along, your friend will slump lower and lower in his seat until you worry that he will pass out in the cab. You know from experience that once he's out, he's out. You will prod him. You will say in a loud voice, "Wake up!" He will jerk up for a moment and then slump back down. You will ask him in a loud voice, "Do you want to go get pizza?" He will shake his head no. You will ask him in a loud voice, "Are you all done for the night?" He will nod his head yes. You will ask in a loud voice, "Do you want to come over to my house then?" He will nod again. You will ask the cab driver to take a left instead of a right and head towards your house instead of towards the pizza place. A block from your apartment, you will tell the cab driver, "Here's good. You can let us out here," and you will hand him some money as you scoot your friend out of the car and onto the sidewalk. The cab will drive away. It will be somewhere between two and three in the morning.

You are tired and you are drunk and it has been a long day. You will take your friend by the arm and tug him towards the hill up to your house. He will stand still on the sidewalk and look confused. He will tell you he wants to go to his girlfriend's dorm room. You will be exasperated. You will wonder why he didn't say something before the cab drove away. There are no cabs here. You just want to go to bed. It's so fucking late. You will tell him the cab has left, there are no cabs. You will tell him he can crash at your apartment. Your apartment is right up the hill. You will tell him it's somewhere between two and three in the morning and he should just crash. You are tired. Drunk. It's been a long day. You will see all of these things in him, too. He will be worse off than you. But he won't move. He will sway for a moment and then he will say he will walk you up to your apartment and then he will go to his girlfriend's dorm. He will take your arm back and lead you up the hill. You will roll your eyes. You can't believe how stubborn he is. You will tell him it's somewhere between two and three in the morning and ask if his girlfriend will even be in her dorm, if she will be awake, if she will let him in so late. He will say he doesn't know. You will sigh. You will roll your eyes again. You will insist that he crash at your apartment. It's late and it's been a long day and you're both drunk and tired. It's somewhere between two and three in the morning. You want the day to end without you worrying that he has passed out in the street somewhere. You think he's being ridiculous. You have been in lots of fights with him lately. You will add this ridiculous behavior to the list of recent ridiculous behavior.

Out of the blue, he will say to you, "I will only stay over if we're going to fuck." You will laugh because you think he's kidding. He's such a kidder. He will not be kidding. He will say it again. "I will only stay over if we're going to fuck." You will tell him you will not be fucking him that evening. You will tell him that is an absurd thing to say. You will tell him that your roommate is away so her bed is free or there's a comfortable couch or there's half of your bed that can be shared without any fucking. You will tell him it's late and you're tired and you're drunk. You will say you have to work in the morning. You will say that fucking isn't part of your friendship. He will say, "I will only come up if we're going to fuck." He will say, "I really love you. I have loved you for a very long time. But I'm not ready for you to be my girlfriend." He will say, "But I really love you. I love you a lot." He will say, "I have wanted to fuck you for a very long time. I really want to fuck you." He will say, "I will only come up if we're going to fuck. If we're not going to fuck, I am going to my girlfriend's."

You will not know what to do. You will not know what to say. You will choke on his words. You will look into his eyes and see he is at his most honest. You will be standing two inches from him, your faces will nearly be touching. You will realize his arms are around you. You are so tired, so drunk, so unprepared for this. You will say, "I love you, too, but we are not going to fuck." You will say, "Our friendship isn't in the greatest place right now as it is. Sex is a very bad idea." He will not be daunted. He will say, "Then how about a blow job?" You will say that would not be any better for your friendship. He will say, "Yes, but can we fuck anyway?" You will say no. You will take a step back. He will stand before you, so drunk, so drunk, and he will look you over carefully from top to bottom. He will say, "You have amazing self control. And you look really very lovely this evening." Then he will turn and slouch away down the sidewalk. You will stand with your arms folded across your chest and watch him until he is out of view. You will go inside then. You will go to bed.

You will not know how this night has detonated your already fragile friendship. You will find out about that later when in two days he will fist pump you and say, without explanation, "I'm not mad at you." And you will find out even more two days after that when he will write you an email saying, "I know you brought me back to your apartment to seduce me. I know you want me but I want my girlfriend. I will never want you." He will write, "I don't want you as anything more than a friend. I never will." He will write, "Everyone knows you are in love with me, but I am not in love with you." He will write, "I hope we can still be friends, even though you are in love with me and I am not in love with you." Your insides will fill with ice when you read this. Your eyes will fill with tears. You will be astonished.

You won't know what to do next besides defend yourself. You will defend yourself. You will try to save face. You will try anything to fix this. He is your best friend. Isn't he? You will try to stop shaking. You will wonder why he remembers everything backwards. You will tell him you don't understand. He will say, "Geez, my bad." He will say, "I guess I got it wrong." You will accept his lukewarm apology. You will say you can still be friends. You will believe you need his friendship. You will believe he needs yours. You will think things will be OK.

Things will not be OK. You will not know this is only the beginning. But you will learn.

Written in 2011

About the Author

Sarah Wolf earned her MFA in Creative Writing from Emerson College in 2005. She is the author of several books, including *Neverland, Ohio*, *Sobriety (And 49 Other Short Stories)*, and *A Somerville Love Story*, and she has written something every single day since January 1, 2011. She lives in Cleveland Height, Ohio. Visit wolfstarpres.com for more information.

www.ingramcontent.com/pod-product-compliance
Lightning Source LLC
Chambersburg PA
CBHW070019260626
47159CB00005B/1882